SO SHALL YE REAP

By
ROG PHILLIPS

I0616856

ARMCHAIR FICTION
PO Box 4369, Medford, Oregon 97504

DIRE PROPHECY OF THE ATOMIC AGE...

There was an invisible atomic fire going on in the Earth's atmosphere. An atomic fire that was started by the first few atom bombs in the mid-1940s. Slowly this atomic fire was spreading over the surface of the planet. It would eventually reach a lethal breaking point. A point that would soon reduce human population to prehistoric levels. With this grim knowledge in hand, the government began the construction of giant underground cities that would allow at least some of the world's population to survive. The question was...who would be allowed to live and who wouldn't?

This grim look at the Earth of the future is an unforgettable masterpiece of science fiction, and the quintessential work of Rog Phillips.

CAST OF CHARACTERS

JERRY CHADWICK
Nuclear physicists don't usually get to meet the President, let alone the premier of Soviet Russia—but he did.

ALEX TOPANOV
He was a brilliant scientist, but perhaps too brilliant for his own good. It was hard living with the discovery of impending doom.

JOHNNY DAVIS
Getting a major news scoop was all that mattered to him—and he'd pay through the nose to get it.

OLLY CHADWICK
A dedicated scientist in his own right, yet often overshadowed by the brilliant accomplishments of his brother.

LOWAHTHY
Apart from being telepathic, the lack of eyes or a nose seemed to be a dead giveaway that he wasn't your average Joe.

RON
He was given a chance to live a life of perpetual comfort, but all could think about was catching and eating his next cockroach!

CATHERINE TOPANOV
She was essentially an all-American gal. Little did she know that her father had discovered the most terrible secret of all time.

AUTHOR'S NOTE

Prophecy is a game played seriously by some, a gift sought seriously by others, and the stock in trade of certain classes of seers and "spirits." Yet what is prophecy?

He who prophesies correctly gains a certain air of authenticity and infallibility. The spiritual adviser, for two dollars, says, "A dark man is coming into your life. You will have three children and be married three times." The gullible female believes it. Didn't she pay the two dollars?

She meets a very nice fellow and marries him; but in the back of her mind is the ominous, infallible prophecy, "You will be married three times." So—one day she and her husband have a quarrel. And she says to herself, "Since it's coming sooner or later anyway, it might as well be now." So she leaves him. Maybe the husband won't let her get a divorce, so she has to kill him to let the prophecy come true. She's caught and hanged, and has to re-incarnate to fulfill the prophecy. But she DOES fulfill it, come hell or high water. After all, it was a prophecy, wasn't it?

Then there's the guy who wants a little fame and maybe he has ambitions about being proclaimed wise above all other men. He isn't too smart. He doesn't have the knack of getting bright ideas. Prophecy appeals to him as the sure road to what he wants. So he collects prophecies, sees how they have come out so far, keeps the ones that have proven infallible to date, coordinates them, and writes a book on prophecy. He even believes it himself. And you can buy it right now. Oh, yes! There are dozens of small frys like this, competing for top honors in the field of prophesying gloom, death and taxation. They all seem to make a living at it, too, one way or another.

Above the charlatan and the seeker after the cloak of infallibility, on a plane by himself, is the person like Oswald

Spengler, a serious, industrious scholar, who masters the whole of world history, coordinate it into one consistent pattern, and by means of this proven pattern, which he has systematically derived from our past, predicts the general trends of the future. His "Decline of the West" is a monument to intellectual industry for which the Germans have always been famous. It is worth real study.

On the same plane, but perhaps on a more practical basis, is the man, H. G. Wells, who long before his recent death, had proven himself many times over as a fairly accurate prophet. So accurate have his prophecies been in the past, that I have often suspected Great Britain of basing her foreign policy on his books as they came off the press. It would be quite funny, I think, if it were ever proven that the lineup in the First World War was what it was because H. G. Wells had predicted it would be, and not the other way around: that his insight into world affairs had enabled him to accurately estimate the lineup.

In everyday life we have the practical prophet; the man who sizes up situations and estimates their future states, and adjusts his own affairs to fit into the future to his monetary advantage. If he becomes powerful enough he gets to the point where he can even compensate for errors by adjusting affairs and molding the future to his ends.

But that ceases to be prophecy. In the popular mind prophecy must predict change. Something different. A weather prophet who predicts sunshine tomorrow when it is sunny today is not considered a prophet. If he predicts rain tomorrow when there is no chance of rain, and it rains, he is a prophet.

The man who publicly prophesies there will be no world catastrophe next year is no prophet. It is the man who warns of dire calamity, who advises you to fill your basement with potatoes this year because there will be a seven-year famine starting next year, who says, "get out of the cities and go into the country and find a small place where you can be self-sufficient because by next year there will be revolution, rioting, and famine in the cities," *he* is the prophet.

In your own mind, isn't that what prophecy means? Suppose you go to a spiritual adviser and he says, "You are married, are going to stay married, will keep on working for about the same money the rest of your working days, and will live to collect a fair part of your old age benefits." Would you feel cheated? Of course you would. That's the way things are *now!* You should get a better prophecy than that for two dollars.

So the prophet, knowing this popular conception himself, tries "honestly" to give you your money's worth.

Underlying prophecy are two radically different basic conceptions. (1) The practical one. Estimation of what can come out of existing things. (2) The spiritual one. "Contacting" the All Knowing, to whom the future is as open as the past.

Under the second heading comes the "Book of Revelations," the pyramids, and a few other prophecies made long ago and "proven" authentic over the past couple of thousand years. Under the first come Wells, Spengler, and others.

But underlying both types of prophecy, I think, is something akin to the first. If a man is really immortal in spirit, and the universe is really limitless and has always existed, there should have been many other planets with intelligent, immortal creatures on them, whose spirits have outlasted the planets on which they first came into being, and have seen the birth and death of many hundreds and thousands of planets since then.

If such is the case—and there is a book called "Oahspe" which asserts it to be so—then what we are going through today is old stuff to them. With the experience gained from observation of thousands of races going through what we are in today, they would be in a position to know with pretty fair accuracy what things will be like here, not only for the next few years, but for the next few thousands of years. Especially if they can influence the course of events to any extent.

All of this brings us up to a very intriguing point, which forms the basis of this story. Suppose that in spite of all their know-how and experience SOMETHING UNFORESEEN HAPPENED? Or suppose that on the thousands of worlds they have had experience with, there were two separate ways things could go?

Suppose that at a certain stage of the game they could say with certainty that there were two different paths future history could take? They could prophesy accurately up to the branch and then GUESS which way we would go. Just as you could prophesy that a man getting ready to flip a penny would flip it—then guess whether it would come down heads or tails.

Or, suppose that in their observation of thousands of planets they were confident about which way things would go, but SOMETHING NEW happened. Something that had never happened before. SOMETHING SO STUPID THAT THEY DID NOT CONSIDER THE POSSIBILITY OF INTELIGENT HUMANS OVERLOOKING IT? BUT IT HAPPENED.

What would they do? That is hard to say. Assuming they had our welfare at heart, considered us blood brothers under the skin, and so forth, they would probably do what they could to help us meet this unforeseen future successfully. But they would be handicapped by the certainty that all their nice prophecies, which were going to be borne out to the letter, would be proven false, and they would be discredited.

That is all a nice field of speculation. If these spirits saw the thing that was going to happen before it happened they would naturally try to prevent it. Maybe they couldn't stop it at the source. Then they would try to bring public pressure to bear against it happening. If that failed they would have to make the most of things. Maybe they would throw in a new prophet. Maybe they would discard prophecy and just try to get over certain basic ideas to help tide us over, by inspiring some "campaign." Maybe the whole thing did happen once, long ago, and they might "inspire" some writer to set down what happened then, so that we would have that "history" to draw on in the crisis just before us, assuming there *is* a crisis.

However it may be, we have an intriguing problem. What single thing, which has already happened, could put the entire human race in a fix it couldn't undo, which would threaten our very existence?

It *could* be that that irrevocable act hasn't taken place yet. It could be that I am "inspired" to write this story so that IT WILL NOT HAPPEN. It could be that there is no possibility of such a situation arising at all. Assuming for the sake of argument that the idea for this story came to me as inspiration from some spiritual source, the story itself is pure imagination. So far as I know, the idea for it is also the result of imagination. So let me say now that THIS STORY IS NOT PROPHECY. *The possibility upon which it is based is only a possibility because I don't know whether it is a fact or not.* If it turned out to be actuality the story might come true. If it turned out to be impossible, the story could not possibly become true.

Be that as it may, for the sake of a good plot, I have assumed it to be true; that already we have irrevocably done the deed, with no chance of undoing it, and that the human race is doomed, unless— But that's the story.

In real life, it might be a good idea if we really find out whether this story MIGHT come true. *Right now,* if it isn't too late already.

—ROG PHILLIPS.

PART ONE

CHAPTER ONE

RON sat on the curb, his small bare feet in the gutter, eyes aglitter with intense alertness. Beady, faceted eyes appeared in the gloom, several feet down the circular well that yawned at his feet.

He stopped breathing, hoping that his smell would entice the insect out of its hole. Firmly grasped in his right hand was the metal hook with which he hoped to secure his prey and drag its squirming body out onto the pavement. Then he could eat.

Thick chunks of delicious white meat would be torn out from under the rock-hard, exo-skeletal casings of its legs. Delicious, creamy juices would drip from its carcass, which would satisfy his thirst and save him the long trip to the lake.

So he waited, breathless, for the giant cockroach to emerge. At his back, rising a full twenty-four stories, was a brick building. Over his head in the street was the gloomy structure of the El tracks. For this, although Ron did not know it, was the loop in Chicago, 2196 A.D. All he knew was that in some one of these dark entryways along this street he had been born, his mother writhing in the agonies of birth, while some other woman watched.

He knew that because he had seen many babies born, and was himself a father. His mother was dead now. She had died when he was three years old. She had been an old woman when he was born. At least thirteen. And no one lived more than fifteen years ordinarily. But there had been no severe Geig storms for several years, so lots of the old people had lived an extra year or two about that time.

The cockroach hooked its front legs over the edge of the hole and sniffed at Ron's feet. He knew it was aware he was a human. The only question in its mind was whether he was dead or not. At the instant experience had taught him was just right he hooked the creature in the thick of its back and braced his legs for the tug of war. It was soon over. He had the cockroach on its back on the pavement and was tearing its legs off, one by one, so that it could not escape.

No sooner was a leg torn off than a new one sprouted from the open wound. If Ron cared to wait, in a few hours this new sprout would be a new leg. He had done that once and found that the meat of the new legs was too soft and tasteless. It grew too fast and did not have the firmness that only days of exercise could give it.

With the creature helpless, he pounded a leg against the concrete sidewalk until the shell broke. Then he tore out big hunks of the quivering white meat and sank his firm white teeth into them. This cockroach was full-grown. Over two feet long. More than a meal for him.

In his eight years of existence he had never seen larger ones. Every year they got larger!

FROM the gloom of the street opening to the building at his back, two female figures emerged timidly. Strong in their minds was the time, two short weeks before, when Ron's third wife had emerged too soon and caused him to lose his prey. He had thrown her after the escaping cockroach, to fall screaming down the shaft of the sewer opening, food for the myriad giant insects that multiplied prolifically beneath the streets.

Betty, the younger of the two—six years old—reassured by Ron's ignoring of their advance, darted forward first and seized one of the legs lying beside the cockroach's quivering body.

The fast growing embryo that pushed her stomach out to alarming proportions made such demands on her body that her digestive system could barely supply her needs. In fact, in the five months from gestation to birth, the embryo would make such demands that she would emerge from the ordeal with very little flesh and no fat left.

Amy, older by two years than her fellow wife, and consequently more cautious, waited until she was sure Ron would not get mad, then, laying her two-months-old man-child on the pavement where he could lap up the juices of the dripping cockroach-nourishment her undeveloped breasts could not provide—she seized one of the legs, cracking it expertly against the curb.

Finally, their appetites satisfied, the three crept back into the protection of the building, Amy carrying her child with her.

There they watched idly as other cockroaches and the dangerous newts crept out of the sewer opening and cleaned up the mess they had left. When they departed there would not even be a smell left.

Ron glanced worriedly at his Geig. Its needle presaged a storm. It had been hovering in the pink area on the dial all day. If it crept into the red, or even went up a little bit more, he would have to lurk in some dark basement for days until the storm passed. Sometimes a wind blew the storm away in a hurry, but not always.

Right now there was no wind. The air was hot and humid. It felt like steam against his skin, and rivulets of sweat trickled down his naked skin, leaving streaks in the dirt.

If the Geig storm came, and there was no wind, it might last for weeks. Then many, many people would starve, and lose their minds and go out into the streets. Then when the storm passed the streets would be littered with the dead and dying, their skins seared pink, large areas turning white and falling away, until they died. Then the cockroaches would come out of their holes and drag the bodies back down with them.

The cockroaches always multiplied faster after a Geig storm. But when the supply of human corpses ran out they would get hungry and dangerous, and their meat would get tough and thin out, so that one cockroach would not be a full meal for three or four people.

When there were no Geig storms the normal death rate of the humans supplied the right amount of extra food for the sewer dwellers above what they got from the rats and smaller insects that lived with them. These wandered in from the surrounding country where they lived on vegetation mostly. Curiosity brought them.

The cockroaches never left the city. Humans sometimes did, although Ron never had. There was a legend of an Opening. What this Opening was, no one seemed to know. It was the answer to all their troubles.

The Geigs wore out in time. They would last three or four lifetimes if they weren't dropped. At the Opening you could lay your old Geig on a stone and it would disappear. After a while another would appear in its place. A bright shining one with a smell of banana oil and bakelite.

There was supposed to be a big door at the Opening. Legend had it that about every three generations the door opened and giants came out and took someone in with them. Ron didn't believe this. Someday he would go see this Opening for himself. All you had to do was keep going west. If you went far enough you would leave the buildings behind and eventually come to the Opening. *If* it existed.

RON kept his eye on the Geig while his food digested. Betty and Amy slept. The baby crawled exploratively around them, never going far.

Imperceptibly the needle crept up toward the red. Finally Ron woke Betty and Amy. They followed him through the inner hall of the building to an opening that led downward. In a few hours Ron would creep back up where it was light with his Geig and see if the radiation concentration had lessened any. But first he would sleep.

Betty or Amy would keep awake. One of the three always had to keep awake. They had the building to themselves, but someone might come. Sometimes Geigs were lost. Then the unfortunate loser would try to steal somebody else's. And sometimes when females were scarce the other men would try to steal wives.

Usually, though, there was no trouble. A man guarded his Geig with his life. And the woman problem was generally the reverse—a man had to drive away wandering women who had no husband or he would have more mouths to feed than one cockroach would satisfy. Then work became doubled. No man cared to take on the responsibility of killing six cockroaches a day if he could satisfy his reproductive urges and only have to kill three of them. He would have to kill three anyway, just to feed himself, since the meat did not keep.

Ron stretched himself out on the basement floor at the edge of the light coming down the stair well. In less than a minute soft snores told that he was asleep.

Betty slept too, shortly, her childish face relaxed.

Amy held her man-child in her arms, rocking slowly back and forth, humming a little tune. The baby watched the way her nostrils flared as she hummed. Then it put its small hand to her lips and gurgled delightedly at the feeling of vibration the humming produced. Although only two months old he could understand most of the words his elders used. In another month he would start walking a little, and using a few words himself. At six months he would be advanced as the three-year-old of two hundred and fifty years before. If he weren't he would die of neglect, because his mother would be unable to look after him and satisfy the demands the next baby would be making on her body.

He would probably die anyway. The average woman produced at least ten babies during her lifetime and yet the population never increased. That meant that eight and a fraction babies never grew up.

Amy smiled at the gurgling of her baby.

"You want me to tell you a story?"

The baby nodded, so she began.

"Once upon a time, long, long ago, there was a nice giant who lived down under the road. He would look up through the road and watch all the little boys and girls, so that if they did anything bad he would know about it.

"When they were good he would chase the roaches up out of the holes so that the good little boy's papa could get them. When they were bad he would stop up the holes and then the bad little boy's papa would not be able to catch any roaches. Then everybody would be hungry. When they got very hungry the papa would drop the bad little boy down the hole and then the giant would chase the roaches up the hole so that the papa and everybody could eat.

"When a little boy is very good and grows up into a very good man like your papa, then sometimes the giant comes up out of his own hole and takes the good man back down with him and then he grows up to be a giant himself, so that he can watch the little boys and girls through the road.

"But if he doesn't, the very good man will still go down and live with the giant when he dies, and then grow up to be a very big giant anyway. And the bad little boy, when he dies will go down into the hole the roaches come out of and be chased by the newts."

RON had awakened toward the last of this story and listened, a smile of amusement on his lips. Now he rose impressively and approached Amy and her baby. With a casually formal stiffness he took the child's hand and said:

"Hello, John."

Amy smiled and tears came to her eyes. Tears of happiness. Her baby was now christened, its future assured, her own status as a wife made certain, and—everything would be all right.

It was a ceremony. One of the few. A girl was driven from her family circle when she was old enough to mate. She wandered through the streets, alone and helpless. It took a man to catch a roach.

She would lurk near the family circle of some man, and when he caught a roach she would dare his wrath and steal some of the dead roach after the rest had had their fill. If she was not driven away she stayed, ready to run at the first frown of displeasure. Often she was tossed down a hole. Sometimes she was tolerated for a few days and then driven away.

If she was lucky she eventually found a man who would let her stay in his family circle. But she still formed no definite part of it. If she did not soon become big with child she would be driven away anyway. If she had a child, she still did not know if she was acceptable. But when her man named her child, it was the unwritten law that henceforth she was his wife until death.

Often her first child would be a freak. Then she would certainly be condemned and chased away. So it was a big event in Amy's life. Now she was what all women MUST become or perish before they are ten: a successful mother.

Ron crept up the stairs to the top, his eyes on the Geig. It crept up almost to the red. Outside it would show in the deep red. This was a severe storm. He dared to look hastily around the corner wall of the stairwell, along the hall into the street.

Dust was swirling lazily outside. Wind! In a few hours the Geig storm would be gone. With a satisfied grunt he pulled his head back. In that second he had looked, his face had begun to smart. He rubbed it briskly.

Betty was groaning in her sleep. She began to grind her teeth in pain. The sound was sharp and painful to the ears in the intense quiet of the basement.

Ron picked up John, his first child, and sat on the bottom step playing with him. Amy watched her fellow wife sympathetically. After a while the baby came—a girl. Its eyes were open, a good sign. It would be a normal baby. If its eyes had been closed it would have been a throwback, a freak. It would have taken too long to grow up. And Ron would have thrown it down a hole and driven Betty away. Maybe he would have thrown her down a hole too. The cockroaches always hung around holes where they got food. And Ron had to be practical. If he did not feed the cockroaches human food once in a while they would not be eager to come up and sniff at his feet and get caught.

After Betty recovered somewhat, Ron again went up the stairs. This time the Geig stayed in the lower pink even in the hall. So he went back to the hole at the curb. As he sat down he looked up and down the street, hoping he might see a corpse he could toss down the hole. It had been three days now since his hole had been fed. Pretty soon the roaches would leave and concentrate around some other hole. It took an hour to catch one this time.

Betty ate the lion's share. Her baby lapped the white juices beside that of Amy. It would be all right.

The meal finished, Ron started west along the street, and Betty and Amy, after giving each other a puzzled look, followed him closely, carrying their babies on one hip.

Ron had made up his mind. He was going to see for himself about this Opening. His Geig was still good. It had been new with his father, so it would be good longer than he would live. It was just curiosity.

Before long they left the security of the tall buildings and the el tracks. Now, occasionally, they passed the bodies of people who had been caught in the Geig storm, their flesh an evil white. Some of them still writhed in the throes of death.

Ron ignored them and Amy and Betty kept close to his heels.

WHEN it got dark they sought the protection of a building. There was a family in it, but the man was old. Over twelve. The man glanced fearfully at Ron, and when Ron showed no signs of hostility the man soon lost his fright and became friendly. He, too, had lived in the loop in his younger days. When he began to get old he had been driven away by the younger men, as all old men were. The loop had the most roaches, and it also gave better protection against the Geig storms.

When it got light again Ron started on. Betty and Amy followed closely. At a distance, a five-year-old girl followed them cautiously. Ron had smiled at her as he left. This was almost enough invitation, but a cautious nature kept the girl at a safe distance. If Ron had not chased her away by afternoon, it would be safe to close the gap between her and Ron's family.

Occasionally the procession passed some building still standing, with a group of women and men lurking inside. Most of the buildings had caved in long ago, however, and the standing buildings with their inevitable populations of child adults became fewer and fewer as the day lengthened.

If a person of nineteen forty-seven had been suddenly transported into the picture, he or she would have been shocked beyond description. Chicago had become a children's city, the buildings falling apart, and filth piled high in the streets.

This race of child-adults was not so much the product of a rapid evolution as a brutal weeding out, a survival of those who could fit into the specialized conditions, which were becoming more specialized each year.

The weeding out had left only those males that could reproduce by the time they were six or eight years old. Then, they appeared no more grown up than a naked, dirty ragamuffin of ten or twelve from the poorer tenement section in any twentieth century city. Actually, the only physical changes wrought in them during the two and a half centuries of change were the compressing of ten or twelve years growth and development into eight or ten. Most of this was accomplished before birth, since the normal baby was now born with its eyes open and quite often with some of its baby teeth.

The shortening by three months of the period of pregnancy was not so much due to evolution as to the richer supply of growth hormones found naturally in the six to ten-year-old mother. Motherhood came early. The ravages of environment made early motherhood a vital necessity, for long before maturity would be reached the body would succumb to the continued searing of lungs and tissue by radioactive oxygen and carbon, not to mention all the other radioactive isotopes, whose concentrations were increasing daily.

In another fifty years Ron's descendants would be gone from the face of the earth. And the cockroaches that enabled them to live, rich with their white meat, very much like crab in taste and appearance, and with their creamy white juices, rich in vitamins and hormones, would be gone, too. A kind nature would see that the food for the children would outlast the children. Wounded and insulted by the rash folly of man, she still watched over him as best she could.

Ron was not aware of the shortness of the time his race had left to it. He was not even aware that man had ever been any different than he was now.

And the man of nineteen forty-seven is not aware of the flexibility of the race of which he is a member. He does not reproduce at the earliest possible moment. Custom forbids it. There is no source of information on the period of pregnancy of six-year-old children. There is no data to supply such information.

But it *is* known that a child of six or eight, if it has had to take care of itself from the time it could walk, has the self-assurance and self-confidence of the adult.

And, though the population left on the surface in the United States in nineteen forty-nine (to meet its inevitable doom in less than three centuries, only vaguely aware of what was in store) numbered over a hundred million, only a small fraction of these were flexible enough biologically for their descendants to survive.

Old age crept down the scale of years until reproduction was in a race with death. Before growth had even started the hormones and regenerative elixirs created in the body to produce that growth were diverted to the grim task of repairing the ravages of harsh, searing air that tore the sensitive tissue of the lungs, deadly missiles in the guise of life-giving molecules that scarred the sensitive cellulose walls of the tissue cells, and fifth-column atoms in the native tissue of the body itself, that squatted in intimate association with unsuspecting companions and bathed them in their poisonous emanations.

THE sun was high in the heavens when Ron stopped at one of the open manholes in the street. Betty and Amy promptly ducked into hiding behind a still-standing section of wall nearby. The five-year-old girl who had followed them stopped half a block away. Ron looked at her, scowling, and pointed sternly toward the place his two wives were lurking.

With a silent exclamation of joy she darted to join them. She was IN!

The hole had yielded up one cockroach in just a few minutes. Two more climbed out during the course of the meal, to join in the repast in a way they had not expected.

Ron took up his pilgrimage with the three girls following, Betty and Amy eagerly getting acquainted with the new girl. Ron listened as the girl disclosed that her name was Mary, that she was five, and that her father had consented to her following Ron because he liked his looks.

Ron's dirty, expressionless back hid the smile of pleasure that lighted up his face at this compliment. A man could not let his women see what reaction they had on him. They had to be kept in their place with an iron hand.

Now the city was behind them. Here and there a house could be seen, still standing, but generally with the roof caved in.

At last he paused. The road intersected a well-worn path that led diagonally across the open fields, winding between the piles of rubble that had once been houses.

This must be the way to the Opening.

Stoically he took the path. His eyes glanced anxiously at the Geig and were reassured by the position of the needle—well down into the pink.

If a Geig storm came now he and his wives would be helpless to avoid it.

The sun was sinking rapidly in the west, its light blinding Ron so that he had to squint, when the Opening came into view.

It consisted of a concrete ramp leading downward at a thirty-degree slope, with high side walls to hold back the dirt into which it sank. At the bottom, about fifteen feet straight down from ground level, it dipped up slightly, with open holes to carry off any water that entered.

It ended against a wall, into which was set two heavy steel doors. A smaller door was set into one of the larger ones. And at one side of these doors, fixed into the side wall of the ramp, was a black shelf.

"This must be the stone where legend says to put the old Geig for a new one," Amy said, standing beside Ron.

Ron nodded in slight condescension, implying that of course he knew all about it. He was a man, wasn't he?

With a mischievous smile tugging at the corners of his mouth he laid his Geig on the table. It lay there for a full minute, then the table tilted upward, revolving into the wall, and leaving a similar surface in its place.

Regret, worry, curiosity, and fatalistic amusement were on his face as he stood there silently, waiting to see what would happen.

CHAPTER TWO

THE quiet *whish* sound signaled the arrival of a carrier through the air tubes. Gar Whitely slid his feet off the plastic desktop to the floor and stood up, stretching. He had been half-asleep for the past hour.

One whole wall of the large room was an orderly design of six-inch copper tubes which entered from both ends of the room and dropped to a long table, partitioned so that there would be no question which tube the incoming rubber-cushioned carriers came from.

He grunted his surprise when he saw which chute the carrier was in. The one from outside. It had been months since any of the surface people had come for a new Geiger counter. He was even more surprised when he opened the carrier and discovered that the counter was not worn out, but in very good shape.

He read off its serial number and looked on a chart that he hauled out of one of his desk drawers. The counter was only ten years old!

"Curiosity!" he exclaimed in amazement. Then he lifted the desk phone off its cradle and dialed a number. Almost instantly there was a response.

"A counter just came in, sir," he said rapidly. "I thought I should bring it to your attention because it isn't worn out. It's only ten years old, and as good as the day it left."

A whistle of excitement came over the wire. After a couple of "yes, sirs," Gar dropped the phone back in place. Then he went over to a large panel and flipped a little toggle switch. A frosted glass square set flush in the panel lit up, disclosing the face of Ron. Gar studied it intently for a full minute.

He shook his head pityingly as he took in the figures of the three girls, and the two babies.

The phone rang, so he turned his back on the picture without shutting it off.

The clipped voice of the man at the other end said: "Give him a Geiger counter. A new one."

With another "Yes, sir," Gar went to a rack and took one out of a box. He dropped it into the cushioned interior of the tube that had brought the old one and pushed the tube through the opening of an outgoing pipe. Then he went back to the screen.

He saw Ron's face light up with delight as the shelf before which he was standing dipped again and a shiny new Geig fell out.

Then Ron turned his attention to the large doors, which also showed in the screen.

The phone rang again. Gar listened for a moment, then said into the phone:

"I'm sure of it, sir. Most unusual. Are you going to bring him in?"

The smile of anticipation that appeared on his face indicated the answer from the other end. As he dropped the phone a second *whish* indicated the arrival of another tube. This time it was the daily paper.

A third *whish* brought his lunch from the kitchen tube. Gar carried the lunch and the paper to his desk and relaxed. The paper was mostly comics. The front page carried nothing but news, however. The transpacific bores were only eight hundred miles apart now. Mesmer had solved the gene pattern of the cantaloupe, whatever that was, and figured out a series of crosses of the melon and cucumber groups that would create it.

Radiation seepage had been detected in the Montana area. That meant that the source of entry would have to be found in the automatically sealed off section, and after it was stopped the section would have to remain in sealed quarantine for two years to see if any particles had entered. Too bad. Copper was the big need, always.

Grange's new composition would be heard on the seven hundred band at eight o'clock. Gar made a mental note to listen to it. It was reputed to be very good. He liked all of Grange's music anyway.

Nothing much in the news. Gar turned to the comics and bit into a sandwich. He didn't care much for liverwurst, so he hastily opened his thermos of coffee and poured a cup to drink with it.

WHILE he read he kept an eye on the panel viewscreen. The other eye, figuratively speaking, read the comic strips. To Gar comics were literature, romance, and adventure. The highest expression of man's imagination.

His favorite character was Xan, the cosmic doodlebug, who, in fiction, had formed the earth by collecting the dust and debris of space and shaping it into a ball. Xan was a loveable sincere stumblebum. He had fallen in love with a human girl and was making pathetically grandiose plans to roll her up in a planet-sized ball of her own. However, he was stymied for the present by the fact that it was against the law for him to bore to the earth's surface without a license.

For over a week now Xan had been getting the old runaround, being sent from one department to another to get a license to bore a hole. Since he traveled through the solid earth by eating the rock in his way, digesting it, and excreting it as a firm, impenetrable lining to the passage he made, he unwittingly went in the directions and to the places that his human friends wanted opened up. When he got there he inevitably received the answer, "No, Xan. We don't have the authority to issue you a license to bore to the surface. But we CAN issue you a license to bore through to such and such location, where, we feel quite sure, they CAN issue you a license to bore to the surface."

And Xan, his huge, worm-like body busy day and night boring, boring, boring, spurred on by the hope of getting a license, directed by his laughing human friends with fictitious licenses to bore in certain places, thwarted by insistent protests that it's "against the law" when he wandered off his course, loved a girl whom he could never see because he had no eyes.

SO SHALL YE REAP

He loved her because her thoughts were beautiful to him, and in his mind's eye he imagined her to be a cute "little" cosmic doodlebug, a wee hundred or so feet long, and a mere wisp of an eight or ten feet thick, with the very daintiest of retractable legs, and the most luscious of rock-wrecking lips.

RON examined the huge doors to the Opening, his new Geig with its strange, delightful smell clutched firmly in his hand. He was being very foolish, he knew. Darkness would come long before he could get back to the buildings and their protection from Geig storms, even as it was. And yet his curiosity made him linger.

Then, just as he was turning to leave, the small door opened and a giant stepped out, enclosed in a shining, transparent bubble. He towered at least two feet above Ron's four-foot figure. In his blue eyes lights danced merrily. Instinctively Ron liked him and trusted him.

"Come inside, son," the giant said in a deep, booming voice. Something stirred deep within the soul of Ron. He had never before heard such a deep, rich voice. Normal human voices to him were the high, shrill voices of boys who died of old age in their middle teens, years before their voices could change in timbre. Yet some racial memory, some instinct, coupled with subconscious feelings of loneliness and longing for the strong adult protection and love that he and his fellows had never had, welled up within him. He dropped to his knees, not knowing why, and bowed his head.

Betty, Amy, and Mary, their eyes round and large with awe, anxiously looked at one another for mutual guidance, then followed Ron's example.

The giant, tears glistening in his eyes, stooped down until his head was even with Ron's. He reached out a cellophane-encased hand and gently lifted Ron's head, smiling at him.

"You don't need to do that, boy," the giant said. "I'm not a god. I'm just your big brother."

Ron thought this over. Suddenly he grinned.

"Not brother," he answered. "Brothers always fight."

Ron rose to his feet. The first feeling of awe at seeing the legendary giant was passing and his curiosity was reasserting itself.

The open doorway promised adventure and mystery, and the giant's words, spoken when he had first stepped out of the Opening, finally penetrated.

Motioning his wives to follow him, Ron stepped past the giant and entered the Opening, that mysterious place that legend, handed down from generation to generation by word of mouth, pictured as the home of the giant.

Inside, a long, uniform tunnel stretched endlessly in both directions, to the right and to the left as Ron stood with his back to the door.

Directly in front of him was a large thing, divided into sections. The giant closed the door and motioned Ron and his three wives to step into the thing. The girls waited until Ron had stepped in and examined this strange object. Nothing happened, so they timidly joined him.

The giant stepped into the end section and sat down. He looked back and motioned the four to also sit. When they were seated he pressed a stud and the strange thing began to glide swiftly along the passage.

Ron had never seen anything move except living creatures and the dust in the street when the wind disturbed it. This was magic! He didn't liken it to the magic of the needle in the Geig that could tell him when the Geig storm came, because that was not magic. That was something everyone knew and used, although no one had ever wondered how a needle could tell such things.

This was something different. There was no feeling of movement, yet the walls and the road slipped by many times faster than they would at a fast run. He barely had time to get over his first instinctive fright when the thing stopped.

The giant said, "This is a car," and climbed out. The car had stopped beside a door in the passage wall. He opened this and stood aside for Ron to enter. Ron was over his fright. Common sense told him he had nothing to fear.

HE ENTERED a large room in which there were many of the giants. One who seemed to be the leader stepped forward and said, "My name is Oliver."

"Mine's Ron," Ron answered. "And this is Amy, this Betty, and Mary." He pointed proudly at his oldest baby and said, "This is my son, John."

Oliver bowed gravely. He knew these child people and their customs quite well, since he had spent a good part of his life studying them with various instruments. He knew that they never shook hands, and that a handshake would mean nothing to them. He also knew that Ron had not introduced the other baby because it had not yet been named. He knew by the way Amy stood confidently beside Ron while the other two girls stood a little to the side that Amy was his only accepted wife.

He also knew they must have a terrific odor, but his cellophane covering saved him from this, although its purpose was to shield his body from any contact with radioactive isotopes which he knew were being thrown off with every breath the five surface humans expelled. When he left this sealed section of the upper tunnels his transparent covering would be washed thoroughly before he entered the main section. Every square inch of it would be scanned by a super Geiger counter which could register the presence of half a dozen radioactive atoms.

"We invited you to come in for the night," he said in a reassuring tone. "It's too far back to the city for you to get there tonight."

Ron said nothing, but gave a boyish grin to show that he had heard.

"When you leave we will give you some things to take with you," Oliver went on. "But we would like to know why you brought your Geig when it is still good?"

"I don't know," Ron said. "I didn't believe the legends and wanted to find out if they were true."

"Are you satisfied?" asked Oliver.

"Yes," Ron said slowly. "Except—will I come here when I die if I'm good?"

"Well, now," Oliver said, laughing, "If that's what you believe, I wouldn't be surprised if you do."

One of the other men now spoke up.

"How would you like to stay here and live with us giants?"

"Gee," Ron exclaimed. "I—I don't know. Would I grow up to be a big giant too?"

"That's hard to tell," the man replied. "You might not like it. You couldn't get any roaches down here to eat. You would have to eat what we do. It might make you sick," He smiled.

"It might be worth it," Ron said. "Back in the city there is only catching roaches and watching out for Geig storms. I think I'd like it…"

OLIVER BERG sat at his desk, fountain pen in hand, filling out a report. It had been three months now since Ron and the three girls had come.

In that three months Ron's adjustment had been very poor. The report told the whole story. Appetite—very poor. Radioactivity—lessening. Mental state—strained. Homesick.

If only something could be found that would absorb Ron's interest. Something must be found, or Oliver would have to let him go. Back to the satisfying thrill of catching a cockroach three times each day. Back to the all-purpose food that Ron had lapped from the filth of the street a few hours after he was born, and tore with his baby teeth when he was only six weeks old. Terrible as such a life might seem to Oliver, raised in the comforts and science of the underground cities, they were home, mother's cooking, and life to Ron.

"It's so hopeless and tragic," Oliver muttered. As president of the Humanitarian Society he had fought for a program to rescue and rehabilitate the remnants of the race left on the surface for the past twenty years.

Twenty years! The people then, the little children who had to be grown people and raise families when they should be just starting to school, those little people that had lived above when he started his fight for them were all dead now. A new generation had replaced them as they died, one by one, of old age at the age of fifteen!

At the beginning, when the chosen few millions had quietly gone underground, leaving the unsuspecting billions on the surface to their fate, there had been too many to accommodate in the living space carved out of solid rock, deep under the surface, by atom-powered boring machines.

Now there were not too many! But with the problem of numbers solved by the increasingly harsh environment man had unwittingly loosed upon his children's children, a new problem had arisen. The racial one. Weeding out of all those who could not fit the new conditions, speeding up of the generations until they sped from the cradle to the grave at two, three, then four times the speed at which they should, had resulted in a different race that bred true. A race that was ready for reproduction and the responsibilities of adulthood when only six or seven, even when they were taken below the surface away from the environment that had been responsible.

Richard Crane, president of Michigan University, under the lake, had stated the case only too accurately. He had said, "The question is not whether we should save those now living on the surface. The question is only partly whether we *could* return them, as a race, to the parent race; and that is doubtful indeed. The question, mainly, is whether we should permit our noble and just humanitarian instincts to preserve a race that can only be a constant threat and sore spot to our own children. A race whose individuals die of old age before they can possibly learn anything other than the most elementary of subjects. A race whose members could only fit into our economy in a menial capacity because they haven't time to become specialists. A race that would inevitably resent its place in the scheme of things and revolt.

"Our great nation was founded," he said, "on the principle that all men are created equal. Let's analyze what that means. If we force ourselves to allow the race on the surface to die out, then a century from now ALL children will be born equal, with an equal life expectancy and equal opportunities. If we give in to our pity for those left to the mercies of the surface environment, then a good part of those children born a century from now will have a life expectancy too short for anything except reproduction. Logic tells us the course we should take."

Oliver had answered him with the inevitable replies; that the surface race could be brought below and segregated into colonies by themselves, with teachers and leaders sent into their colonies to guide and aid them, that eventually they might again become normal. But the arguments were weak, and he knew it as he made them.

IT WAS not as though there really were *two* races. There was only one race, and a part of it had become a misfit. It was the old problem of sterilization of the mentally defective to prevent them from having children, in a new form. It was based on the premise that you can't murder a child that hasn't been conceived.

There had been movements that advocated a systematic program of sterilization of the surface people. There had been a movement that advocated the stopping of manufacturing of Geiger counters for the surface people, so that the environment would do its work of extermination quicker. These movements fought without success, while the little Johns were born to grow up to be Rons before their time, squatting at sewer holes, catching cockroaches so that their infant wives could bear children. And in fifty years, unless the surface race could make further changes so that a two-year-old could reproduce, they would be gone from the face of the earth.

Oliver was no longer fighting to save the race on the surface. He was fighting to save just one boy. He loved Ron as a father loves a son. Ron's quick, mischievous smile, his curiosity, so rare now in surface people, and his unusually high intelligence, had won him a place in the hearts of most of the people who had seen him.

And yet, in his heart Oliver knew that Ron would be much happier back on his own corner in the Chicago loop, king in his own little world, killing three giant roaches each day with an eye on his Geig while he dismantled the insect so that his kingdom could eat.

What did he have to replace it? Perhaps five extra years of life. Or five less, if he didn't survive on other foods than the one he had always lived on. And what of his children? Should they be sterilized? And what activities could be found for Ron to replace his cockroach hunting?

AND WHAT WOULD BE RON'S REACTION WHEN HE DISCOVERED THAT THE GIANTS WERE LIKE THE FREAKS THAT WERE TOSSED DOWN THE HOLES ON THE SURFACE? Ron didn't know yet that the giants were born with their eyes closed, and that, according to his standards, they were still helpless when they should be running around and looking out for themselves.

It was a hopeless problem. Oliver sighed deeply and returned to his report blank.

IN spite of Oliver's gloomy thoughts, Ron was thoroughly enjoying himself. To be sure, he often thought of the city and felt homesick for it. But he knew that if he insisted he would be allowed to go back. They had told him that several times. He wasn't a prisoner.

The queer-tasting foods often made him sick, and the milky fluid they provided for his babies was very weak, but it was provided in huge quantities so that the babies were never hungry. He didn't mind getting sick except when he couldn't keep the food down. And there were so many fascinating things to see and learn.

Moreover, with the problem of food and Geig storms solved, he was thinking seriously of returning to the city and bringing back several more wives. As soon as he thought the opportunity to broach the subject was right, he intended to do so.

He was confined in a large room with one wall made of glass. The giants came and talked with him on the other side of the glass. After he had been there several days they brought him a cellophane covering. He put it on and was taken through a room where water washed all over his suit. Then they took him on a long journey in a fairyland that beggared description.

Miles and miles of roads. He saw and heard things beyond imagination. Things that were flat and smooth to the touch—television screens, they were called—seemed to be living, solid parts of the world. Most marvelous of all, he actually saw himself as he stood outside the opening when he first came. He saw himself meet the giant for the first time. *Newsreel,* they called it.

Nothing seemed impossible to these giants! And Ron had grown used to miracles. He had even grown to expect them. He and the three girls spent hours each day exploring the strange things that split open in thin layers. Books, they were called. There were queer, fascinating little figures in the books that could say things that the giants understood, and claimed he could understand, too, if he wanted to learn. Already he could recognize several of these little figures and name them. But the most fascinating thing about books was the pages that were like the television screens, only the world they displayed didn't move.

And the pencil! Ron, Amy, Betty, and Mary spent hours each day making marks on paper. Marks that awed them even more than those in the book, for those in the books were made by the giants who could do anything, while those that the pencils left were made by them, which proved they were akin to the giants.

Ron's adult dignity would have been wounded to the quick if he had known that these marvels were merely the equipment given to kindergarten children. He would have readily admitted that he could never hope to equal even the least of the giants in wisdom and ability to perform magic, but would have denied hotly that he was subnormal.

Human values always seem absolute, but are forever relative. The highest pinnacle of genius of one generation of man becomes the study of school children in the next. The accomplishments of the outstanding men of one period soon become everyday commonplaces. Abilities considered rare in one century become common in the next.

The surface man of 2196 A.D. tossed his "freak" offspring to the cockroaches and newts and drove out its mother to fend for herself because the "freak" if allowed to live, would be completely helpless for a third of its lifetime. The "cave" man was permitting the surface man to die out because he could not live long enough to learn more than the bare rudiments of civilized society.

OLIVER and many of the other giants knew these problems and their inconsistencies. The guilt of their ancestors, who left most of the race to a horrible fate so that the seed of the race could live, to again people the Earth in that far off day, two thousand years away, when the Geig storms would be no more, weighed heavily on their spirits.

It didn't matter that no other course could possibly have ensured the preservation of the race. It was wrong to steal quietly into the depths of the earth and safety, without even warning those left behind of their inevitable fate. But of what use would it have been to warn them? Where could they go?

Would they have passively let a few steal into the earth so that their children would live, while their own would die a horrible death in generations to come? Do people in a burning building stand quietly, letting the flames lick at their clothing and sear their flesh so that others no better than they will have room to walk comfortably to safety? If they do, they are brave and worthy to live, while the selfish few who escape should die in their place! A dilemma!

Would part of the race have accepted sterilization so that there would be no children to face the horrible future, while permitting a selected few to go below and sire the future man? Would *you?*

Who were the men, back in nineteen forty-seven, who appointed themselves gods of the destiny of man? Who decided what part of the race was to be preserved? Who made the decision to leave the rest of mankind in ignorance of its fate, to breed children whose descendants would squat above sewer openings in dead cities and cunningly snap the insects whose equally cunning ancestors had lived on the refuse of man's dinner table? And why did this have to be? Why? WHY?

Let's leave for a time the story of Ron—Ron, with his quick, loveable grin, and the proud smile on his seven-year-old face when he introduced his son, John, to the giants, those normal descendants of ours. Let's leave the story of Amy, and Betty, and of Mary, that pretty, five-year-old girl who ran after Ron to become his wife and bear him children—and die at fifteen because the scar tissue in her lungs would produce oxygen starvation and the delicate membranes of the walls of her body cells and blood vessels would become too thick to allow the waste products of metabolism to escape.

Ron and his wives are happy with their pencils, making scratches on paper that delight and mystify them. The suffering they experience when the food the giants give them does not set well on their stomachs cannot compare with the suffering of the soul of Oliver, with his knowledge of the past and of the future to come, when the descendants of Ron—his last descendants— are burned through and through by the lethal intensity of gamma rays from the air they breathe.

Maybe Ron will stay with the giants and learn to read. More likely he will tire of the magic of the giants and return to the hole in the street, down on the loop in Chicago, where he can catch the wary cockroach and sink his teeth into the white, raw, insect meat that his body craves, to be king of his own little world, and die.

Let's go back. Back to nineteen forty-seven when it all began... Let's look at those who DARED to decide the destiny of the race, and said, "You, and you, and you, can go below and sire the children who will eventually be able to come back up," and who said, "You, and you, and you, and all of *you*, can stay, and sire children who will live on the filth in the sewers and die with their flesh falling off in white, lifeless chunks, or of old age when they are yet children."

What could have happened that made such decisions necessary? Was it the result of some diabolical scheme of a madman, bent on conquering the world? Or was it some mistake somebody made? Something overlooked until it was too late? Some oversight?

Let's go back and see.

PART TWO

CHAPTER ONE

ALEX TOPANOV dropped the much-worn, yellow pencil from tired, numb fingers. For several minutes his eyes rested on the last of the many sheets covered with figures and scribbling that littered his desk. As he looked, his face seemed to age visibly.

Finally he rose and walked slowly over to the window that overlooked a large part of the campus; but he did not look at the beauty of the flowers and the smooth green lawn, nor at the almost fragile beauty of architecture that was embodied in the library building with its tower, set in a triangle of buildings whose laced granite windows swept almost from the ground upward for seventy feet. His eyes rather sought the sky above and beyond the tower.

They seemed to concentrate on something that was hidden in the calm, blue, almost holy purity of the heavens, and in the filmy white clouds that floated lazily in that sea of blue.

His eyes held an infinite regret and a sadness at the realization that he was seeing something that someday no man would see again.

He alone, in all the world, knew that. The realization that he must tell the world caused his shoulders to sag and his head to drop on his chest.

It was all there on paper, on his desk.

He had gone over it too many times for there to be any possibility of a mistake. The known value of the atmosphere and its contents, the total volume of water in the oceans and rivers and lakes, and the rates and half-lifes of the substances involved. There was no getting around it and no way to undo it.

As he stood there, head bowed, he remembered a story he had read years before of a prisoner of war on a desert, who had been condemned to death by his captors. Having been granted one last request before the spears would run through him, he had asked for a glass of water.

When it had come he had looked fearfully around at the enemy soldiers. The captain had said.

"Do not fear that my men will slay you before you drink. You have my word as a soldier that none shall harm you until you have drunk every last drop of water in that glass."

"Your word?" asked the prisoner; and as the captain nodded his head the prisoner tipped the glass, spilling the water onto the hot desert sands. Then, smiling, he had said, "If you can gather the drops of water from the sands of the desert I will willingly drink them, but until you do you cannot kill me without losing your honor." His life was saved.

"It would have been much easier," Alex Topanov said softly to himself, "to have gathered those drops of water and put them back in the glass than it would be for us to undo what we have done."

He pulled himself together with a visible effort and turned back to his desk. Carefully sorting the papers laying there, he put them into a folder and placed it in a pocket of his leather portfolio. He was zipping it shut when the door opened and his daughter, Catherine, came in.

She was wearing white shorts with a loose, white blouse. The skin of her long, shapely legs, her arms, and her face was tanned a rich, smooth brown that seemed the darker because of the light color of her hair which hung in loose disorder.

In one hand she held a tennis racket, idly letting it swing at her side. The other hand held the door open as she said:

"Come on, Dad. We'll be late for dinner if you don't hurry."

"There's no hurry," Alex said, his eyes averted to the 'folio as he slowly put it under his arm, hiding the knowledge his eyes would betray if he looked directly at his daughter.

37

"Yes there is," she replied laughingly. "You know how the housekeeper always goes into a tantrum when dinner is delayed. And you've put her off schedule twice already this week. The first thing you know she'll be quitting."

"Catherine," Alex said. Something in his voice sobered her.

"What is it, Dad?" she asked.

"Would it all right with you if we went back to Poland?" He spread his hands deprecatingly. "There are lots of nice boys there, too, you know. And I would like to go back home."

"Why, Dad! You old silly!" Catherine exclaimed. "Are you working on some new death-dealing device? The last time you wanted to go back was just before they dropped the bomb on Hiroshima. You *never* want to go back to Poland unless something is troubling you. What is it this time?"

"Oh, nothing," Alex said hastily. "Nothing at all. I just thought—maybe—you might want to go. Why of course there's nothing wrong," he went on in forced merriment. "After the atom bomb what else *could* there be?"

"Nothing *I* could imagine," Catherine dismissed the whole subject. "Here. Let me carry your 'folio. You're getting slower every day."

SHE took his 'folio from under his arm and marched out of the office. Sighing hopelessly, he followed.

In the hall Jerry Chadwick, the young nuclear physicist waited impatiently, his tennis racket pressed to white-sweatered side under his muscular arm, the crease in his gray slacks unspoiled by the two hours of exercise on the tennis court.

"Hurry, Dr. Topanov, or you'll lose your cook," he greeted Alex, a broad smile on his clean cut face. The neckless, short-sleeved sweater set off his head and shoulders to good advantage.

"Hello, Jerry," Alex said in a tired voice.

"Catherine almost beat me today," Jerry said as the three walked down the hall to the exit.

"What do you mean, almost," Catherine said indignantly. "I won one set and we had to play over for you to win the second. If we had had time to play a third I would have won, easy!" She wrinkled her nose at him.

"Jerry," Alex said soberly as they descended the broad steps at the front of the building to the walk that led across the campus. "Will you go fishing with me tomorrow?"

"Yes," Jerry answered pleased that Dr. Topanov would want to go fishing with him.

"All right. Be over at the house about five, then, so we can get an early start."

"Will we take a lunch?" asked Catherine.

"You're not going, Catherine," Alex said after some hesitation. "I just want to relax with no one along but Jerry."

"Well, I am, too," Catherine objected, pouting.

Alex chuckled. "Go ahead and pout," he teased. "You're left out in the cold on this trip."

"I think you're a couple of meanies," Catherine exclaimed, but there was a thoughtful look in his eyes. "Something's up," she thought to herself. "I'll worm it out of Jerry when they get back."

"How's Olly coming with his book?" Alex asked Jerry, changing the subject hastily.

"Too well, if you ask me," Jerry answered, a worried frown appearing on his face. "He spends most of his time on it. When he isn't writing he's in his lab conducting experiments. He has one whole section of his lab piled with what he calls environment chambers now. And each one is working."

"He still thinks he can find the first life form?" Alex asked wonderingly.

"He not only thinks so," Alex said emphatically, "But he is positive of it! That's what those environment chambers are for. But I think he's on the wrong track."

"Hmm," Alex said softly.

The three had come to the parking lot and were climbing into Jerry's red Buick convertible.

When they were seated Alex said, "Suppose we stop at Olly's lab and see if he will join us for dinner. I'd like to listen to his ideas some more."

"Okay," Jerry answered, "but I doubt if he will tear himself away from his work long enough to eat any more than a hasty meal at the corner cafe."

Jerry brought the car to a stop at a red light. Alex signaled the newsboy on the corner and bought a paper. As the car again went into motion he spread out the paper and glanced over he headlines.

HIS eyes came to rest on the item about the detection of radioactives from the Bikini explosion over Los Angeles. The report said that they had been carried in by the wind, but would have to be a hundred times stronger to have any effect on life.

His eyes dwelt broodingly on the news item, while Catherine and Jerry engaged in small talk, unheeded by him. After a few moments Jerry brought the car to a stop at the curb and hopped out.

Five minutes later he returned, followed by his brother, Olly. The resemblance between the two began and stopped with the general structure of the head; the same forehead and hair, the same cheekbones and the same cut of chin and jaw line. But there the resemblance stopped. Where Jerry was tanned, and his expression that of habitual enjoyment of life, Olly's pale face pictured only the suffering and introvertive intentness of expression of the physically inferior.

As he crossed the sidewalk to the car his left arm was drawn up against his chest, the withered hand bent sharply at the wrist. His right hand gripped a cane which he used to help his dragging right leg along. His unpressed suit had cigarette ashes liberally spotted against its dark surface.

His half-closed eyes came to rest on Catherine and stayed there as he climbed into the car. Alex had slipped into the back seat while Jerry was gone, and Olly took his place beside Catherine.

"Hello, Olly," Alex and Catherine spoke together.

"Hello," Olly smiled at each in turn, then settled on Catherine again. He had never dared to ask her for a date. His only moments with her were like these, when he was included on something with his brother. He didn't mind too much. He knew that it was best this way. Catherine could never look at him the same way she did his brother. All there was for him in life was his work; but sometimes it was hard to reconcile himself to being a cripple.

Catherine's eyes took in the lines of fatigue on his fine, ascetic face.

"You've been working too hard, Olly," she said softly.

He shrugged his right shoulder and smiled resignedly.

"What else is there for me to do," he said. "Should I drag myself around a tennis court?" He glanced at the two rackets on the floor of the car.

"No," Catherine admitted, "but you could take a book and go sit on the campus in the sun." She regretted her words as they came from her lips. Biting her lip she turned to Jerry.

"Don't forget—" she stopped. She had been about to remind him of their date to play doubles with some friends on the uptown tennis courts Sunday, but somehow everything she said when Olly was around seemed to hurt him.

"Forget what?" Jerry asked glancing at her briefly and then returning his eyes to the job of driving.

"The latest Bing Crosby record," she went on as if that was what she had been intending to say. "You promised to get it for me when you went down to the record shop."

Jerry kept his eyes straight ahead and said, "Okay." Not having made any such promise he knew what Catherine had been thinking.

"Damn Olly," he thought to himself bitterly. "If there were only some way to get him out of his self-pity and feeling of inferiority..." He was really a fine brother. Before the motorcycle accident that had injured his spine he had been the better of the two. But since then he had grown more and more

41

to feel himself unwanted and a burden on the world. He would have to snap out of it someway or pretty soon he *would* be a burden on any company he was in.

JERRY had picked Alex up at six A.M., and they had reached the river a little before seven thirty. Alex had brought along his 'folio. Catherine had been up and had still wanted to go along. She had accused her father of being childish when he insisted on taking his 'folio along. He had been adamant on all counts. The only part of Catherine he permitted to come was the lunch she had prepared for them in the hopes that that would make her father relent.

The argument over the 'folio had created a mild curiosity in Jerry. Only mild because he knew that Alex had been working on something lately, and might want to do some thinking on it in the peaceful atmosphere of the river.

So it was with some surprise that he heard Alex say, after their early lunch.

"Jerry, my boy, I want you to go over some work I've been doing and see if I've made any mistakes. But before you look at it I want you to promise that you will not say a word about any of it to anyone at all. No one."

"Why, of course, Dr. Topanov. You know I wouldn't do a thing like that," Jerry answered with considerable surprise and hurt.

"I'm sorry," Alex apologized, sensing Jerry's hurt. "I didn't mean to imply anything. You will see after you read these papers that there was a very good reason. But I want to impress on you that you *must* keep what you learn a secret. You may not think so after you read them. You may think it's your duty to humanity to rush out and inform the world. I felt that, too, at first. But I have come to the conclusion that it will take better heads than yours or mine to decide what is best to do with what I've discovered."

He opened his 'folio and slowly took out the papers he had worked on for the past few days. Wordlessly he handed them to

Jerry. Then he lay back and closed his eyes wearily as Jerry began to study the equations and written words on the unglazed yellow sheets of paper.

It took Jerry a half-hour to skim through them. Then, a worried, puzzled frown on his face, he took out his pencil and began to check the mathematical work.

He looked up once and said; "These figures are what you had the whole department working on two weeks ago, aren't they?"

Alex nodded without opening his eyes or changing his relaxed position.

Finally, Jerry laid the papers and his pencil on the riverbank beside him and stood up, flexing his back to get the stiffness out of it. Then he squatted down, picked up a pebble and frowningly threw it into the stream.

In his mind's eye he saw the waters of this river flowing to the ocean, evaporating in the rays of the sun and drifting inland as fleecy clouds, to fall again on the mountain side and drain into the river, and once more drift back to the ocean.

It was an endless cycle, the cycle that made life possible on the earth. Now, as he watched, he saw that it had suddenly become something sinister—a death cycle that would forever END life.

HE KNEW only too well that the conclusions Dr. Topanov had reached were correct. They should have been obvious from the day the Curies had first isolated radium. But they had been overlooked. Jerry smiled wryly. It was a human failing to overlook certain things. A human carried his thinking up to a point where he had his desired objective and then dropped it.

One city dumps its sewage into a river that passes through another city. That city pumps its drinking water from the river, and has epidemics of disease. Even after the germ was proven to be the cause of disease, cities fought against laws protecting the purity of streams because it meant spending money for sewage disposal plants, and money for chlorination plants to purify the drinking water. People, including him and Dr.

Topanov and Roosevelt and Einstein, never thought of everything. They always stopped thinking at the point where they had what they wanted.

And now—Jerry raised his eyes to the blue sky showing through the trees. His eyes held the same look that Alex's had held the day before as he looked through his office window at that same sky. A hurt, helpless, hopeless resignation. A resignation that knew nothing could be done.

It was a look that thousands of pairs of eyes would hold soon. Millions.

Alex looked silently at the back of Jerry's upraised head and knew what thoughts were running through his mind.

"It's a terrible thing to contemplate, isn't it, Jerry," he said softly.

"Damn it, Alex," Jerry said, throwing another pebble in the stream. "Isn't there *some* way of undoing it?" And even as he asked he knew there wasn't.

"Maybe we could evacuate the planet and settle on another," he finally suggested.

"Where?" asked Alex. "You can see now that the same thing must have happened to Venus. Nothing else could explain her unexplainable blanket of clouds that hides her surface. Mars? Maybe it happened there. That would account for her loss of atmosphere and water. One of the moons of the larger planets? Maybe. But we don't even have one ship that could leave the earth yet, let alone enough to evacuate the whole population in three centuries."

A horribly sick feeling was growing in Jerry. He saw himself marrying Catherine and having children, and the children growing up and marrying. He saw the inevitable consequences; his descendents in three centuries facing the merciless sky, to be burned and cooked by the Gamma radiations that poured out of the atmosphere in ever more lethal concentrations.

No! He couldn't let that happen! And yet he must not tell anyone about this. He knew that, too. If he told one person that person would tell others. Eventually the whole world would know. And then there would be panic, riots—and if some refuge from the coming cataclysms were found, the millions would trample themselves to death in a mad struggle to be the ones saved from extinction!

The problem was too great for one person, or two. And it could not be kept secret.

"What do you plan on doing, sir?" Jerry asked in a subdued voice.

"Now that you have verified my conclusions, Jerry," Dr. Topanov said in a firm voice, "when we get back to town I plan to wire the President for a consultation. I'll lay the problem squarely in his lap. Then *he* can decide."

"That's the best thing, I guess," Jerry said. "Should we go? Somehow I don't feel like fishing any more."

Without another word the two men, one young and with most of life yet before him, the other old and bent, with all of life behind him, rose and climbed up the bank. With them went the secret, known now to TWO men.

IN SEATTLE the evening editions of the papers were rolling out of the presses. People were glancing at the clocks, impatient to leave their work and hurry home. In thousands of hamburger joints people were idly listening to the voice of Bing Crosby, or the funny music of Spike Jones, from the juke boxes. And none of them knew.

In three centuries some of these places would still be standing. But there would not be so much as a fly buzzing around a customer. Nor even a customer—not one. There wouldn't be even a weed growing in the vacant lot by the drugstore, nor an ant crawling across the sidewalk.

And five hundred years from now some space traveler, coming near the solar system, would make notations in his logbook.

"Second and third planets covered by dense cloud layers. Periods of revolutions unknown because no surface landmarks are visible through the clouds."

CHAPTER TWO

ALEX and Jerry stopped at the telegraph office on the way back home, and sent a telegram. It read:

"Secretary: Must see President at once. Urgent matter. Most urgent. Wire or call. Also arrange travel priorities. Dr. Alex Topanov."

Since Alex's work had been outstanding in the construction of the atom bomb, and it was so well known in the President's secretarial circle, there was no question but what the telegram would be acted on immediately.

Neither man spoke as they left the telegraph office. Finally, the silence still unbroken, Jerry pulled the car to a stop before Alex's house.

Catherine saw them pull up, and ran down the sidewalk to meet them.

"How was fishing?" she asked, her eyes looking at them with a shrewd, penetrating analysis.

"We caught six nice rainbows," Jerry grinned. "But your father got four of them. He seems to read their minds and know just the flick of the wrist that will make the bait most enticing to them."

"I know it," Catherine said, laughingly. "I've seen him operate. He should write a book on fish psychology."

"Maybe I will, some day," Alex joined in. "A man has not truly become a philosopher until he understands the psychology of a rainbow trout."

"Do you mean a salesman could hook more prospects, if he knew how to hook a fish?" asked Jerry.

"I venture to say he could," Alex said. "After all, the technique is much the same in both cases."

Alex had been unloading his equipment. Jerry remained in the driver's seat, and as the three laughed at Alex's remark, Jerry slipped into low gear, and said.

"Well, I'll be running along. See y'all later."

"Jerry!" Catherine shouted. But the car sped down the street, with no sign that Jerry had heard. Catherine watched the fast vanishing rear bumper, puzzled indignation in her clear blue eyes.

"Well I like that!" she exclaimed. Then turning indignantly to her father. "Dad. What have you said to Jerry that would make him act like that?"

"Nothing," Alex said, puzzled. "I'll have a talk with him tomorrow and find out what's wrong."

"No you won't," Catherine exclaimed. "I won't have you meddling in my affairs. If I can't handle them myself I certainly don't want you playing nursemaid."

She angrily picked up the wicker fishing basket with the trout in it and stamped lightly into the house. Alex followed her, bewildered by her outburst.

MEANWHILE Jerry drove the car in the direction of his and Olly's apartment. His mind was in a turmoil of indecision. He had "cut" Catherine on the impulse of the moment, then regretted it at once. He should have gone on as if nothing were wrong. Now he would meet an angry, demanding Catherine the next time he saw her, if he knew anything about her at all, and he could not explain his action without giving away the secret that was not his to divulge.

He parked the car in the garage, and found Olly in the apartment, for a change, a triumphant look on his face.

"Jerry," Olly exclaimed, when Jerry entered the door. "I've found it at last."

"What?" Jerry asked absently, tossing his hat on the bed and starting to unlace his boots.

"The right environment for development of the first life form," Olly cried excitedly. "If you remember the Graham

Theory of the origin of life, you recall that he said the first life form must be either a hydroxicarbon or a hydrocarbon molecule of the repeating variety. That is, it builds up in such a way that each section is like every other section in it, and that when it gets so long it breaks off, so that the two segments go on building up independently."*

---

* In an atmosphere of methane gas, hydrogen and steam, with no other substances present, introduce a single molecule of methyl alcohol, or methanol. Under certain conditions it might be possible that the reaction would be as pictured in the following equations.

$$
\begin{array}{ccc}
\text{H} & \text{H} & \text{HH} \\
\text{HCH} + \text{HCH} = & \text{HCCH} + \text{H}_2 \\
\text{O} & \text{H} & \text{OH} \\
\text{H} & & \text{H}
\end{array}
$$

Then

$$
\begin{array}{cccc}
\text{HH} & & \text{H} & \text{H} \\
\text{HCCH} + \text{HCH} = & \text{HCH} + \text{HCH} \\
\text{OH} & & \text{O} & \text{O} \\
\text{H} & & \text{H} & \text{H}
\end{array}
$$

If, further, the production of methanol from methane were practically impossible when the methanol is not present, and it is produced easily when methanol is already present, the mixture of methane gas and water vapor may be likened to a simple food, and the methanol molecule to a simple life form which reproduces in it. If a mixture of ethyl alcohol, CP, and water, CP, can be subjected to temperatures or rays or catalysts that make it break down into methyl alcohol, the case is proven.

The same principle of a substance being necessary for the production of more of the same substance in a given medium, applied over the whole field of organic chemistry, would account completely for life.

—Nature of the Universe, *by R. P. Graham.* (not yet published)

"Yes, I know all that," Jerry said absently. "He couldn't prove it, because, although it was obvious which hydrocarbons should be the logical ancestors of all living substances, he wasn't able to discover the right conditions—" A look of startled surprise appeared on his face.

"Olly!" he exclaimed. "Don't tell me that you have actually discovered *the* environment and that you have ordinary methyl alcohol reproducing its kind...?"

Olly nodded, grinning delightfully.

"Well I'll be darned," Jerry exclaimed. "Now you'll be the next Nobel Prize winner or I'll eat my shirt."

A shadow passed over his face. The memory of what he had learned that day was a dark, stormy cloud hanging over the future. Olly had found the proof that life is a perfectly natural type-reaction in chemistry, just like all other chemical reactions except that the reaction was built upon the same kind of molecule that would be produced as the product.

But what difference would it make in three hundred years when there were no more people to know about it? Jerry forced these thoughts out of his mind and followed Olly down the back steps to the laboratory, to see what had been going on.

Olly pointed to two large glass tanks, completely enclosed. Inside each was an identical cloud of steam and glass encased thermostat.

"In this one," Olly explained, pointing to the one on the right, "there is no alcohol at all. None put in at the start, and not a trace now."

"In this one," he said triumphantly, pointing to the one on the left, "I put in one drop of pure methyl alcohol two weeks ago. Now there are strong traces of alcohol in it. Not only methyl, but ethyl, and several other alcohols, bearing out the broken chain hypothesis..."

"What's the environment?" Jerry asked, now as excited as his brother.

"Just plain carbonated water, CP, and nitrogen. I found that my failure in my first attempts was due to the oxygen I left in the environment chamber. This time I carefully ran carbon dioxide through until all the air was replaced by it. The oxygen had the effect of disrupting the alcohol molecules at boiling temperatures, and killing the experiment."

"Now you can go ahead with your book and have something to back it up," Jerry said, a glad light in his eyes.

"And will it be a honey now!" Olly exclaimed.

THE sound of the phone came down the stairs. Jerry took them two at a time. It might be Dr. Topanov. It was.

"Hello. Jerry?" Alex's voice came over the phone faintly.

"Yes," Jerry replied crisply.

"Uh—Jerry," Alex said with some hesitation. "I got a telegram from Washington. They seem to want us there about something. They didn't say what it was."

From the tone of Alex's voice, Jerry gathered that Catherine was listening, and her father didn't want her to guess that he had requested the interview with the President. He instantly fell in with the deception.

"From Washington?" he exclaimed incredulously. "I wonder what could be up?"

"I'm not sure," Alex went on with evident relief. "It must be important because they have already arranged plane priorities for us to go in the morning. Can you be ready to pick me up and get to the airport before seven-thirty?"

"Yes," Jerry answered. "I'll have Olly with me. He can bring the car back home when we leave."

"Fine," Alex said. "Oh, just a minute, Jerry. Catherine wants to talk to you."

"Hello, Jerry," Catherine's voice came over the phone almost immediately. "What was the matter with you that you drove off like the devil was after you?"

"Sorry, Catherine," Jerry answered. "I was worried about Olly. But he was all right. And say, Catherine. He's found the right environment to cause methyl alcohol to reproduce, thus proving that it's the first life form, just like Graham predicted!"

"Oh, that's wonderful," Catherine exclaimed. "Now he can announce his discovery and print his book—and make enough money from it to have an income for the rest of his life."

"Isn't it swell," Jerry said enthusiastically.

"I guess you won't be able to keep that tennis date day after tomorrow," Catharine changed the subject. "You'll be in Washington with dad."

"Yeah, that's right," Jerry said. "Well, I'll see you when we get back, Catherine."

"What's the matter with you, Jerry?" Catherine asked, worry in her voice. "You sound so darn formal. If you're going to give me the gate, say so. You don't have to be so tragic and formal about everything."

"No Catherine. You know I love you," Jerry said pleadingly. "I'm certainly not giving you the gate."

"Something's on your mind, though," Catherine suggested. "I know it's something you and Dad talked over while you were fishing. Can you...can you tell me about it?"

"No," Jerry fell into the trap. "That is, there wasn't anything. At least nothing about you. I mean, it wasn't any that had anything to do with us." He pulled out his handkerchief and wiped the perspiration off his forehead.

"Well, I'll let you go now," Catherine said. "But I warn you that I'm going to expect some answers when you and Dad get back. You aren't going to have any secrets from me if *I* know about it." Then, in a softer voice, "Goodnight, Jerry."

"Goodnight, Cathy," Jerry said, and hung up.

ALEX and Jerry were met at the airport by two young men who looked like college students—except when you looked in their eyes. Then, somehow, you knew that they had killed people, sometime or another, and would do it again with the same matter of factness that a cook in a hash house flips eggs over in a skillet, if it became necessary.

The brightly polished sedan took them quickly to a new-looking apartment building where they found that an apartment had been vacated for them temporarily.

One of the young men said that the President would see them any time they were ready to go. Alex had said to come back in half an hour.

During that half-hour they had freshened up a bit and had a cup of coffee that a midget bell hop had brought up to them on a huge tray after they had phoned down for it. The coffee had been good, but the ice water in its sweating glass pitcher had been much more to the point.

Then the two young men had come back, discreetly knocking at the door. One of them had phoned the White House before they left the apartment.

Alex had been in Washington before, when Roosevelt was alive. Jerry had never been here before. But both were too preoccupied with the coming meeting to notice anything outside the windows of the smoothly gliding sedan.

At the White House the car pulled silently to a stop at a side entrance and Alex and Jerry found themselves hustled efficiently along corridors. Before they knew it they were standing inside a doorway and the President was rising from his desk, hand outstretched, a broad smile on his face.

"How do you do, Dr. Topanov. I've heard a great deal about you and your work and it's a privilege to meet you personally."

Alex shook the President's hand and introduced Jerry.

Now they were standing there, an uncomfortable silence settling over them. The two young men showed no inclination to leave, and there were two secretaries hovering in the background.

"What's on your mind?" the President asked cheerfully.

Alex looked embarrassed and glanced uncomfortably toward the secretaries and the two young men.

"Could we talk with you alone?" he asked finally.

"Oh, come now," the President laughed. "You don't need to fear that anything said in the presence of these men will ever leave the secrecy of these walls—if it needs to be kept secret."

"Mr. President," Alex said with some intensity. "In my judgment, what I have to say should be said to you alone at this time. If necessary, Mr. Chadwick can leave the room with your men, and I will submit to stripping and putting on a sheet so that you can be sure I have no weapons on me. I'm an old man, and you are undoubtedly more than a match for me in a hand-to-hand struggle. If you fear for your safety that should more than satisfy you on that score."

The smile on the President's face vanished abruptly to be replaced by a piercing look as he took in the keyed up tenseness in Alex's figure.

He turned his head toward the secretaries and the two young men and nodded almost imperceptibly. Silently they left the room.

The three men remained motionless for a moment after the door closed behind the departing figures. Then the President returned to his chair behind the presidential desk.

ALEX, his hands trembling, laid his 'folio on the desk and unzipped it, taking out the papers with his figures on them.

"Mr. President," he said, "Here are the figures to prove what I'm going to say. You can have them gone over by others to verify my results, but they will only find out that I have made no errors in my results, unless it is in the dates.

"You'll see after you hear me why I insisted on your men leaving. This is something too vital and too dangerous for just anybody to know, no matter how close to you he is, nor how sure you are he can be trusted."

Alex smiled worriedly.

"I'm not too sure that even you can be trusted with the knowledge, sir. But there is no one else in a position to accomplish what needs to be done, and I couldn't be sure of them either."

"I see that you think you have something of tremendous importance," the President said. "You may be sure that no matter how unbelievable it may sound, I'll give it most serious consideration and not treat it lightly. Go ahead and tell me about it."

"It all hinges," Alex began, "on two things about radioactivity that have heretofore been considered unimportant. Neglecting these two things was an oversight on not only my part, but that of every nuclear physicist since radioactivity was first discovered. That oversight has *already condemned the human race and all life on this planet to extinction in three hundred years.* It may be more or less time than that. That period of grace was arrived at by estimating the amount of air in the atmosphere around the earth and the amount of water in the oceans and rivers and lakes."

Alex talked earnestly for almost an hour. The President listened, at first incredulously, then with dawning realization that here was something beyond belief. A trap that man's blind belief in the fundamental goodness of nature had led him into.

Finally Alex's voice stopped. The quiet murmur of noises from other parts of the building, and noises from the street, filtered into the quiet of the room.

The President stood up and walked over to a window. He stood there, his back to the men in the room, and looked up into the sky. Alex and Jerry knew what he was thinking. They had done the same. And each time they looked, the sky seemed bluer and a little more incapable of doing harm than before.

After a while the President turned around, seeming to jerk himself back to the present with a strong effort of will.

"Of course I must have these figures and the facts they are based on checked over thoroughly," he said gravely. "But I realize now, at least as well as both of you do; the importance of keeping this secret for the present."

He sat down again and drummed his fingers on the surface of the desk, thinking.

"The reporters will be quite a problem," he said, more to himself than to Alex and Jerry. "Not an inkling of this must get in the papers. If your facts hold water we may have to decide to take other nations into the secret, too. Every race and nation should have an equal chance to save itself. There will have to be experts in every field of human endeavor let into the secret. No possibility must be left unexplored."

He jerked his head up and looked at Alex.

"When did you say this would end, so that life on the surface would again be possible?" he asked.

"In two thousand years," Alex said slowly.

CHAPTER THREE

JOHNNY DAVIS was a specialist in his field. He had climbed to the top by putting two and two together where other reporters could only see disconnected twos. Deep down in his heart he felt that he was the guardian of the four freedoms, the protector of the people's rights, and the champion of the public; the uncoverer of secret governmental activity without equal.

He had gotten to the top by being systematic. A firm believer in knowing what you are looking for, he had often said at dinner parties that a hunter must make up his mind what he wants to hunt before starting out.

"If you are hunting for deer," he had often said, "you never notice a rabbit unless you stumble over it. If you are hunting for rabbits you pass by a deer and think it's a tree."

In his little black book he kept lists of things to look for, in the order of their importance as news. At the top of the list was always a date. He never tore out these lists, and they were remarkable in their picturization from month to month of the things that made news.

Heading the list for some time now, were two quite well-known words; atom scientists. The fact that they were there at the top of the list indicated why Johnny was tops in his profession. His well ordered mind could give in a definite order the reasons why he considered them special. First, nuclear science was the most interesting news item. Second, atom scientists hadn't done anything for several months to gain the limelight, so any real news from that direction would be fresh. Third, his infallible news instinct told him that the probability of something popping in that direction was quite great. Fourth, the other reporters were asleep there, so anything that he could get would be a scoop—and he had climbed to the top by bringing in a consistent string of scoops during his years as a nationally known reporter.

He brought his radio program, C.B.D.'s—Candy Bar Delights—the confections that were the "object of my affection" to twenty million of the American public daily. And it provided him with two-thousand dollars each week to bring in his scoops. He used it sparingly, but judiciously, and, as a result, had many thousands of pairs of eyes and ears all over the world constantly on the alert, hoping to get a little of that money.

Whether they were lucky enough to get any of it during one particular week or not, they always received Johnny's latest order-of-importance list, which was something in itself, since they were all local reporters with ambitions.

Over a hundred of the two thousand dollars each week went for collect telegrams that came into Johnny's office from the members of his worldwide, extra curricular staff of reporters. Another hundred and fifty went to pay the salaries of the three—perhaps the only three girls in the United States who had both the looks and the brains necessary to work for Johnny.

Many an editor of a local paper would have promptly fired his best reporter if he had known that orders from Johnny's Washington office superseded his own. Yet, quite often, that reporter gaining a minor scoop, not of national importance, because of a tip supplied by Johnny as his agile mind kept in touch with the national and international pulse, sifting and sorting things as they happened, weighing them in the balance, and picking the half-dozen or so items that he broadcast each day, throwing the crumbs to the local editors via their star reporters.

Sometimes Johnny watched a thing develop for weeks before he "broke" it in his broadcasts. Quite often he paid a great deal of attention to something that seemed significant, only to drop it, file it away for future reference when he found it too insignificant for his tastes.

THE telegram from Seattle was one of two hundred and fifty that the three girls had to read and sort. It merely read, "One two seven thirty transcont. Art." The translation was obvious. "Atom scientists, two of them, by seven-thirty plane to Washington," and the name of the star reporter on the P.I, the Seattle morning paper.

A phone call to the local airport disclosed when the plane would arrive, another call ensured that a local reporter would see what took place when they landed; then the girl laid the telegram in the number one, active, basket, with a penciled notation of her calls. Four minutes and twenty seconds on the telegram, then she went to the next one. As simple as that.

The reporter that watched Alex and Jerry meet the two young men and ride off in the shiny sedan with the special license plates on it promptly phoned Johnny's office. Automatically the girl made two marks on that reporter's score sheet in the card index, which meant he would receive a check within ten days, and called Johnny.

When Alex and Jerry stepped from the shiny sedan to the corridor that wound up at the President's office, Johnny himself was standing in the outer secretarial office. His keen ears heard the atom scientist's voice, pitched high with emotion, as he said:

"Mr. President, in my judgment what I have to say should be said to you alone at this time."

It had been so inaudible that Johnny was quite sure no one else in the outer office had heard it. He was equally sure of what would happen next, so without waiting for more he left. One can't snoop at keyholes in the White House. What Dr. Topanov would say to the President could be found out later.

Johnny found a phone booth and talked swiftly to one of his "boys" in the pressroom for several minutes. Then he called his office and made love to the secretary who answered, giving her incidentally a few terse instructions.

He dropped the whole matter from his mind when he dropped the receiver back on the hook. There were more important things to occupy his mind for the present, such as an afternoon cocktail. He could be reached in his regular haunts.

WHEN Alex and Jerry left the President there seemed to be an atmosphere of subdued excitement in the outer office. Outside, the city noises seemed to have taken a higher, almost electric pitch.

One of the two young men, on the way back to the apartment house, told them about it. Russia had called her British and American ambassadors home "for consultation". For several weeks Russia had been putting pressure on everything at the peace conference. She had vetoed where she could, obstructed wherever possible. Now this.

The buzz of conversation on the streets had a questioning, hysterical tone. Did this mean war? Was it only another episode in a war of nerves? It was anybody's guess.

As Alex and Jerry crossed the lobby to the elevator, snatches of conversation impinged on their consciousness.

"—atom bomb would wipe out the Kremlin within twenty-four hours after they declare war."

"They *have* the atom bomb or they wouldn't dare."

"—be no declaration of war. The first we'll know will be when Washington is bombed."

"What we need is an atom-proof Capitol."

"Yeah. The President ought to get out of the city. We don't have any vice-president."

"It's coming sooner or later, so why not—"

The closing of the elevator door cut it off. Alex sighed heavily as they were lifted at breathtaking speed to the floor of their apartment.

In the apartment Alex said:

"Well, it looks like we'll be in Washington for a couple of weeks, at least. So I think I'll write Catherine before we eat."

He sat dawn at the writing desk and listlessly picked up the hotel pen.

Jerry sat with one leg hooked over the arm of the most comfortable chair in the apartment and listened, broodingly, to the harsh scraping sound of the pen on paper as Dr. Topanov wrote.

He glanced at his watch. It was four-thirty. The plane trip had been tiring. The stopover at Chicago had been a long one. Some mix-up in their priorities. A room had been obtained for them in the Palmer House, but they had only had four hours sleep before having to rush out to the airport again.

He stood up and said over his shoulder to Alex as he went toward the door, "Guess I'll go down to the lobby and buy a paper." Alex merely nodded his head to show he had heard, and kept on writing.

THREE days passed slowly. Alex and Jerry had seen the President again the second day. He had asked them questions, then informed them that several experts in various lines were being called in. When asked what he planned to do, the President had been rather hesitant about answering. He seemed worried.

Alex was stretched out in the comfortable chair, his legs resting on another chair that he had pulled up to use as a footstool. He was reading a magazine.

Jerry had turned on the radio. The program of music ended. There were some commercials. Then the C.B.D. program came on the air. After the standard song commercial, "The object of my affections, is C.B.D. confections, from morn to noon and night," the machine gun voice of Johnny Davis came on.

The first seven minutes, as usual, were devoted to a rapid-fire series of scoops. Then there was the usual intermission for commercials. The second, half of the program was always devoted to Johnny Davis' predictions, most of which usually came true. Jerry and Alex lifted their heads in amazement as Johnny Davis began speaking again.

"Ladies and gentlemen," Johnny's voice rang out over the radio, "I am going to do something I have never done before.

I'm going to retract a prediction I made last week. Last Thursday, over this microphone, I predicted that within ten days Russia would recall her ambassadors to the United States and Great Britain, and that they would stay in Russia. I predicted that there would be a declaration of war within a month, and that Russia would announce a Monroe Doctrine for Europe as the cause for which she would fight.

"I had good reasons for that prediction. The facts on which I based it were from unimpeachable sources. I say now that that prediction would have come true in every particular, just as it has already come true in one respect, with the departure of the Soviet Ambassadors of the United States and England—except for one thing. A new element has entered the picture that did not exist last Thursday.

"So now I predict—that the Soviet Ambassador will return to the United States within thirty days, that there will be no war, and—THE SOVIET WILL DO AN ABOUT-FACE AND WORK IN CLOSEST HARMONY WITH THE UNITED NATIONS FOR AT LEAST THE REST OF THIS YEAR.

"I predict—that there will be a meeting of the big three—in Russia—within two months.

"I predict—that they will lay the groundwork for the setting up of an international police force, the details to be worked out by a commission, which will convene shortly after the meeting of the big three."

"I predict—that an international police force *will* be set up, and it will be in full operation by next spring."

As the program ended, Jerry said with a chuckle, "Can't you just see him if he knew?"

"I predict," Jerry said, mocking Johnny's voice, "That in three hundred years there will not be a creature alive on this planet. I predict—that in two thousand years—if there were any life left anywhere—it could live again on this planet."

Alex laughed mirthlessly. "There's our secret. But I can just see him! He would consider that the peak of his career—to tell the world what's going to happen and prove it so that no one could doubt."

Both men were silent, thinking of that possibility.

"Think of what would happen," Alex went on, suddenly. "Assuming some refuge can be devised against it, where men could exist for two thousand years, until they could again live like we do now, it would have to be for all or for none. The human is so constituted that there would be too many who would say, 'If *I* can't see my children safe from what's coming, *you* can't either.' They wouldn't think of the race, and that they are merely individuals, members of the race, and that it's the race that has to be saved. They would only think of themselves, and that you are no better than they."

"Yes," Jerry agreed, "If all the unselfish people in the world voluntarily relinquished their right to preserve their own children, and stepped aside so that the selfish ones could step in ahead of them, there would still be too many demanding that their children be saved.

"The quickest way to be sure of wars and race extinction would be to let the public know what's coming. And that's what Johnny Davis would do; tell all. Once he found out, nothing would stop him."

"Well," Alex said with relief, "there is no way he can find out. Everything will be done on the quiet. Not an inkling of what is going on behind the scenes will ever reach the papers to draw his attention to us. So we have nothing to worry about."

"That's right," Jerry agreed, and then, as a heartfelt afterthought, "Thank God."

JOHNNY DAVIS stood looking forward, resting on the balls of his feet. His tweed suit looked like it had just come from the tailor who made it, which it had that afternoon. His freshly-shaven features glowed with health as only those who are on top of the world mentally can glow.

His left thumb was hooked in his lower left vest pocket, and his right index finger stabbed at his audience with rapier-like thrusts as he spoke. His audience was the cream of the Washington reporters.

"Look fellas," he said. "There's something on the fire. Something cookin'. I don't know what it is—but we've got to find out.

"My hunch is that it will be the scoop of the century. What have I got to go on? Just this." He paused and his quick eyes darted over his audience.

"We have one of the chief atom scientists of the world come unexpectedly to Washington and go directly to the President. He's met by the President's own boys and Senator so-and-so takes a hurry-up trip home for no reason at all, just to give the scientist a place to stay."

Johnny looked down at his vest, a self-satisfied smile on his lips, at what he was going to say next.

"I'm in the outer office of the President when the boys march Dr. Topanov in to the President's office. I hear him with my own ears order the President to clear the room so he can talk in private. And the President does it! Imagine that. Something so private that even the President's personal secretary and the secret service boys are not permitted to listen.

"What could it possibly be?" Johnny spread his hands in a gesture of puzzlement. "Let's put two and two together. Dr. Topanov is an outstanding atom scientist. The field is the youngest on earth. *Anything* can pop up in it. The atom bomb? Every one dropped is obsolete before it hits the ground."

The assembled reporters chuckled. Johnny grinned, and said, "Pretty good, huh?" Then he frowned to clear his thoughts again.

"What I'm driving at is this; the President is no fool. He's known since early summer that Russia wasn't going to play ball with us. The way Topanov talked he hadn't dropped in to pass the time of day. He gave orders and the President took them without a murmur. So my guess is that Topanov and some of the other key physicists like young Chadwick, who came with him, have been working on something ever since the war, and they've finally got it! What does that mean? It must be something that makes the atom bomb obsolete, at the very least. Maybe something that can wipe out all of Russia at one blow. What happens? You heard my predictions this evening on the radio. If you didn't listen in you're fired.

"I figure that in a few days now—about the time the Russian Ambassador gets home, the American Ambassador will quietly walk up the steps at the Kremlin and hand proof in black and white that the minute Russia declares war we will wipe her out completely. The minute I get a cablegram from Moscow with the word, Caviar, in it I'll know that's happened.

"Then Russia will have to be good until she figures out what to do next. My guess is that she will be *very* good."

"Well, isn't that good?" asked one of the reporters.

"Sure that's good," Johnny replied emphatically. "But wait till you see what comes next. What happens? The President isn't going to be elected next term. Even he knows that. The unions are out to get him. But good. So what will he do? My guess is that while he has the chance he'll see that he gets the job of CHIEF OF THE INTERNATIONAL POLICE FORCE. The only way he can do that is to force it on the world with the threat of total destruction by this new weapon the atom scientists have cooked up, and force the commission to make him chief. Then to hell with the job of President. He can tell the *new* President what to *do...*"

JOHNNY DAVIS was breathing hard with emotion now. He had kept to himself most of the conclusions he had drawn on world affairs for the past year. They were being borne out now. He went on.

"What's been happening during the past few months. Molotov is smart, but not as smart as the American and British diplomats. Do you think it was an accident that Molotov got a seat in the second row behind the British and American delegates not long ago? Do you think that *any* of those subtle insults to the Soviet Union that have occurred during the past few months have been—oversights?

"Almost from the day the President took office there have been subtle digs that goaded Russia on, so that she got the reputation of being surly, warlike, aggressive. For what?

"Don't forget that it has always been the policy of both the United States and Great Britain to goad her *chosen* enemy into being the bad, inhuman aggressor. *That's* what I *think* has been going on. I think the President knew almost a year ago what Topanov was working on, and about how long it would take. I think he timed things very nicely."

"Now," Johnny's voice implied he was winding up his speech, "What I want is absolute proof. I want a scoop that is a scoop. I want, without warning, to bring the American public all the facts; the proof that their President plans on ruling the world! What I want you to do, and all my other boys all over the country, is to keep an eagle eye on every atom scientist constantly. I want to know when each of them so much as scratches his head, and why. And I want to know it within hours so that I can coordinate everything and know what's going on when it goes on—not a week after it happens. I want lines tapped, telegraph personnel bribed, microphones in their homes attached to recorders, infrared photographs and letters steamed open and Photostatted. This is a crusade!"

"What about the do-re-mi?" a reporter asked.

"There'll be plenty of that, too," Johnny said. "Now get going. Work as a team. Some of you cover Topanov and Chadwick. Some of you cover the air terminals and railroads. Some of you cover the White House. We'll use my office as a central clearinghouse, and see that your employer gets enough news to satisfy him. All you'll have to do there is write it down and read it off. But *I* want action."

He walked out without another word. But his forceful personality seemed to linger and dominate the room.

THE presidential yacht slid away from the protection of the shore and nosed its way carefully through the ocean swells.

Alex and Jerry stood on the bridge with the captain, watching the giant seas come toward the ship, slowly and majestically, to pass on either side, lifting the hull and lowering it with a constant, gentle rhythm.

The President was in his stateroom, talking by direct radio scramblephone with his office. Officially he had a cold and was seeing no one, but would talk over the phone from his office when it was important enough. Right now he was talking to one of the senators who had something he thought important to discuss. The senator would never suspect that his call had been relayed to a navy land station and run through a scrambler and broadcast to the presidential yacht.

In a few hours a small boat would pull alongside and take Alex, Jerry, the President, and a few other men on board. Then it would head to a large aircraft carrier that could already be seen on the edge of the horizon, where the men would board a B-25 which would carry them directly to Moscow.

Jerry leaned on the rail of the bridge and was silent. He was thinking of Catherine, and of Olly and his book. He was slightly homesick, tinged with a faint hope that he might die before he got home. In other words, he was seasick. But, as is so often the case with mild seasickness, he didn't know it.

He was very blue in his thoughts. The fact that his name would be immortal—if the race managed to survive that long—because Alex had charitably insisted that the report be called the Topanov-Chadwick report, did not elevate his spirits in the least.

He squared his shoulders manfully. He was facing the issue squarely now. He loved Catharine. If he married her they would have children and those children would have Children, and then his descendants would be living in the last days, when people would cry out in pain and suffer untold agonies from the searing blasts of hard radiation. He could not willingly, with knowledge beforehand be the instrument by which such agony would be brought about.

SO SHALL YE REAP

No—he couldn't. And he couldn't let Catharine know the reason why. The secret was too dangerous for him to take that responsibility. There was only one course open to him. He would have to break off with Catherine and not tell her why. Perhaps he would have to lie to her and say that he didn't love her any more.

He pictured the scene in his mind as his eyes stared unseeingly at the waves.

"Catherine," he would say, "I may as well tell you now as later. I know it will hurt you, but you might as well know the truth. I don't love you anymore."

No. That wasn't any good. He had a sneaking suspicion that she would see through that. He was no good at lying. And Catherine had a genius for smelling a rat. It would have to be something better than that.

He frowned in intense concentration. It would have to be something good. Ah! He had it. Why hadn't he thought of it before? He would destroy her love for him. He would be a cad.

He pictured the scene in his mind. He would stop the car on some quiet country lane. He would make amorous love to her and imply that his intentions were far from honorable. His thoughts turned his face a little red.

Then the horrible thought hit him. Suppose she didn't mind? What would he do then? No! Emphatically no. That wouldn't do. It would have to be some other way.

He sighed miserably.

Alex, mistaking the sigh for impatience, said:

"It shouldn't be long now, Jerry. I see the small boat taking off from the aircraft carrier now. It should be here in half an hour."

Jerry nodded without looking. Alex returned to his conversation with the captain—they were discussing ocean voyages that each had made, and Jerry returned to his thoughts.

What could he do that would be sure to turn Catherine's love to hate? Making dates and then breaking them, or not showing up, would only infuriate her. She would worry about his mental health. She did that when he had once stayed up all night studying and could hardly see the ball on the tennis court the next day.

She had thought he was trying to hide something when he belatedly explained that he hadn't had any sleep. She worried for several days about whether he was having a nervous breakdown or not.

He sighed again. Then glanced quickly at Alex and coughed to cover up the sign.

Suppose he started chasing after every girl on the campus? Gawking would get her if he kept it up long enough.

The only trouble with that was that he would have to spend too much time at it. And Catherine would probably think she wasn't attractive enough and spend a lot of money at the beauty shop and get a lot of new dresses. That would hit Alex's pocketbook. And anyway he didn't think he could gawk convincingly enough to disgust her. At least not enough to make her break off with him.

He sighed gustily this time. It was no use. But maybe he would die before he got back. Then the whole problem would be solved.

A picture rose in his mind. He was sitting in a black touring limousine, riding along a street in Moscow. Suddenly a Bolshevik dashed out and pointed a rifle at his head and fired. He slumped down, his head a gory mess.

Jerry shuddered at the prospect. His eyes wrenched back to his present surroundings. The motion of the boat seemed to be getting more deliberate. It made his eyes jump around a little. He concentrated on that sensation. Yes. It was definite. There was a distinct pressure on the top of his eyeballs when the ship went up, and a distinct pressure on the bottom of them when the boat dropped in a trough.

Funny he hadn't noticed that before. But then the boat seemed to be rocking more than it had. He felt a little dizzy. More like an upset stomach. What had he had for breakfast? The corned beef hash was a new experience. Maybe that was it.

Suddenly he retched.

The rest of the trip was a nightmare to him. The small boat had risen on fifty-foot waves, at least, as it carried him to the aircraft carrier.

The other had been concerned about whether the plane could take off from the deck of the carrier safely. He had silently prayed that it wouldn't, and been disappointed when it rose safely into the air.

The plane had taken a course to the north of the regular lanes, and it had been quite rough. More than once Jerry had been convinced his stomach was above or far below his body.

When the plane finally landed safely at the airport outside Moscow and he had been whisked, along with the others, away toward the city in an open limousine like the one he had pictured, in every detail, he knew with a kind of cruel fatalism that he would not be allowed to die.

So he resigned himself to the slow rocking of the earth, which was almost as bad as the rocking of the plane and the boats had been, and after a while it lessened. By the time the car drew to a stop in front of the hotel where they were to stay he could stand unaided.

THERE followed several days that seemed distinctly unreal to Jerry, and no doubt to Alex, too, although the first half of his life had been spent in surroundings much like these.

Jerry's mind was numbed to sensation. He met and spoke to Stalin. It was a fact in his mind that seemed divorced from emotional associations. For hours he stood or sat uncomfortably in the presence of fabulous personalities.

The king of England, who came at the insistence of the President who would accept no lesser one from the British government, took a personal liking to Jerry. Yet even he, human as he was, remained in Jerry's memory later as only a more vivid detail of an incredible dream.

It took three days for Stalin and the King to completely realize and accept the fact of inevitable doom for all life on the

Earth's surface. Another two days were required for them to catch up with all the possibilities that the American experts had explored. During that time they readjusted their views, as had the President.

They became calm men, coolly discussing the fate of the world together. At once they realized that all short-range problems would have to become secondary. There would be no time to waste in petty, global wars for things that yesterday, and the day before, had seemed of paramount importance.

Power would have to be divided—not for the prestige and commercial advantage it might bring, but for the more facile domination of world events.

World domination by one nation would be suicide for all. Public knowledge of the impending state of affairs would be suicide for all.

A definite plan was worked out in broad outline. The only escape would be underground, in carefully sealed cave cities. They would have to be carved out deep under the surface, in living rock. The alloys, the techniques, were at hand. Boring machines and systems of carrying off the material carved out were the main problem. Constant mutual exchange of information would be necessary.

Methods of choosing and spiriting away the people who were to go down into the caverns would have to be mapped out in detail. The sudden disappearance of millions of people without arousing suspicion among the rest would be a major problem.

It was admitted by England's King and by the President that the life of any man who threatened the secrecy of the project must be forfeit. A new light was thrown on the value of any single human life. Here was a giant, sleeping animal—Man. He MUST not be awakened, no matter what the cost. Out of the womb of the sleeping giant, the egg (from which the future giant—Man, after the death of the radioactive monster—would hatch) must be hidden away in the earth where it could lie dormant until the time it could emerge.

Plans were outlined. Procedures to ensure secrecy were decided upon.

Then, abruptly, the plane was lifting from the ground and boring westward over Sweden, over Norway, and out over the ocean, always far up in the stratosphere, undetected.

There was an awful moment when the pygmy aircraft carrier loomed dangerously ahead. The sudden jar and jerk as the wheels hit the deck and the cable caught the tail hook and held the plane.

The small boat again became a part of the nightmare for Jerry, and was gone, to be replaced by the yacht. Unbelievably it slid alongside a dock. And by the time the long sedans with their smooth, rolling motion had slid innocently into the traffic of Washington, reality had descended with her calm, capable, comfortableness upon Jerry once more.

As if awakening from a dream, he welcomed the honks, snorts, and tire noises of cars in the traffic, as a baby chick welcomes the cluckings of a mother hen. He was back in Washington!

JOHNNY DAVIS was confused. Very confused. For the first time in his life he was confronted with things that didn't stack up. He had evidence—irrefutable evidence—that the President had never left Washington, and equally irrefutable evidence that the President had gone for a cruise in his yacht, had boarded an aircraft carrier, and had taken off in a plane, heading north.

What was this evidence?

First there was his very dear friend, Senator so-and-so, who had called up and TALKED to the President on some very vital matters three different times while the President was supposed to be away. He had called without warning each time and had been immediately connected with the President, without the least delay.

Second, there was the President's doctor who had informed the press on the progress of the President's cold each day, and had been seen to call at the presidential mansion each morning.

Third, there was the statement from one of the crew of the President's yacht, and that man got fifty dollars each time he told Johnny the President had so much as stepped aboard. There was no reason for the man to lie.

Fourth, in confirmation, the statement of the sailor on the aircraft carrier.

To add to the confusion, there was no word from his aide in Moscow. That wasn't too surprising. If the Russians wanted something secret they could easily do it until the reporter came back to the United States.

The actions and movements of outstanding scientists were consistent in only one respect. They came to Washington quietly, and either left as quietly or remained and became grimly uncommunicative.

Switchboard operators in hotels had been replaced by unbribeable, new operators, or had suddenly become upright and honest. Telegraph procedure had suddenly undergone revision, and a new station had been opened. Some (as yet undetermined) code number must route certain telegrams through the new station, and the delivery boys from there were men with guns.

Rooms above and below, and on either side of visiting scientists and engineers were filled with strangers who had a habit of opening their doors and standing in them when anyone passed along the halls.

The scientists themselves could be approached easily enough, and a sizable chunk of expense money was going each week on drinks and food for their entertainment, but they wouldn't talk about their business in Washington, even with the promise that their names would be spread favorably all over the country.

Johnny was quite aware that he could not so much as whisper what he thought of the things that were going on without complete and irrefutable proof of every ward he spoke. But how could he get it?

"I'll have to wait for developments," he muttered disconsolately.

His smile was grim as he left his office for more relaxing things—like a cocktail. He had run up against secrecy before. All he had to do was keep at it. There would be a slip here, a slip there, and he would put them together and get the picture.

He had a reputation that was known all over the world. *Anybody* could send him a little tip, from the President's secretary down to the rear admiral's daughter, and be sure of a sizable reward, and complete protection of identity.

These scientists would go home and talk to their wives, children, and sweethearts. They would talk to their less scrupulous colleagues.

The elevator came and its doors swung open. Just as he was stepping into it his office door opened and one of his secretaries called him back.

Inside, she wordlessly handed him a sheet of paper. On it was an AP release. It said: "George Cramil, reporter for the Associated Press, was killed in an automobile accident while driving from Moscow to Leningrad. His car, going at a terrific rate of speed, plunged off the road into a stone wall. No one was with him at the time."

Johnny crumpled the paper in his suddenly constricted fingers. He paced the floor nervously, his face working in futile rage. George had been one of his few personal friends. They had been cub reporters on the same sheet, years ago.

"You know what this means?" he said, looking from one to the other of his three secretaries. "It means that George knew something."

His eyes darted to the phone, speculatively, then he shook his head.

"No," he exclaimed, as if answering his unspoken thought. "This is too hot to trust to the phone. It might be tapped."

Turning, he left the office.

HALF an hour later he was sitting across the desk from a dignified man with iron gray hair which had too much wave in it to be natural, and with a face that was too masculine to belong to a man who waved his hair.

Johnny was not aware of the inconsistency. He was talking urgently, in a low, bitter voice.

"You knew George as well as I did," he was saying. "*I* think he would have left something to show what he had found out. Something the Russians wouldn't guess. I don't think his death was an accident.

"You've got to send somebody to take his place. Give whoever you send instructions to go over George's stuff with a fine-tooth comb, but not to send what he finds. Keep it to himself.

"Or better yet, some code that takes a series of messages to tell. Something like the first word in the first cablegram, the second in the second, and so on. Then in a week or two we can have the dirt. Huh? Do this for me."

"Okay, Johnny," the man with the iron gray hair nodded his head gravely. "George was one of my best men."

Johnny left his office with a light of triumph in his eyes. Maybe, in spite of everything against him, he would get something to crack this thing wide open.

"If I can *prove* that the President was in Moscow," he whispered to himself, "That's all I gotta do."

CHAPTER FOUR

ORVIS G. OSHIBOSKI wrote his name with slow deliberation just above the line made of a series of short dashes on the official looking blank. The pen point poked through the paper three times, so that the results weren't too good.

It took him so long that he got a little nervous at holding up the slowly marching line of men.

He dropped the pen with relief as he finished writing his name, and followed behind the man ahead of him, his heavy shoulders swaying a little, his flat nose and huge jaw mute testimony that here was brawn, not brains.

The line was vanishing through a door up ahead. In a few minutes he would vanish up there, too. His expression showed that he was a bit nervous. The word examination scared him. But seven thousand a year for a laborer was worth the ordeal of an examination. What puzzled him was why you had to have an examination to get a job as a laborer. What was a laborer supposed to know, anyway?

That question was bothering every man in the line. What was a guy who didn't have any trade supposed to know?

Orvis' friend, Billy Nugent, on the Chronicle, who had argued him into applying for the job, said he didn't need to worry. Billy was a smart reporter. He and Orvis had gone to high school together.

Only two weeks ago Billy had come to his house to talk to him. He'd brought a quart of really nice stuff with him. Orvis had some ginger ale in the refrigerator.

They'd been talking over old times when they were on the football team together in high school. Then Billy had brought out the civil service notice and the application blank.

"Look, Orvis," Billy had said, "seven thousand a year is a lot of dough. Some bank presidents don't make that much. In three years you can own a house as nice as mine, over on the south side where your kids can grow up to be gentlemen like me and earn money by their wits—not have to dig ditches all day out in the sun."

Then he had leaned over close, after glancing out into the kitchen to be sure Mary, the wife, wasn't overhearing anything, and said in a low voice. "You can make a lot more than that. The big boss in Washington, D. C., wants to know what's going on in there. The government doesn't start up the Hanford plant again for nothing."

"Won't that be spying?" Orvis had asked Billy doubtfully.

"Of course not," Billy had exclaimed indignantly. "I ain't working for some foreign power. I represent the press. You know that's one of the things we fought for in the war: *freedom of the press*. And the government ain't letting the press in on this. That's un-American ain't it?"

Orvis had still looked doubtful, so Billy had clinched the argument. "You know me, don't you, Orvis? Am I some foreign b——d? Hell no! I went to school with you when we were kids together. And the big boss agreed to pay you two thousand bucks in cold cash when you tell me what they are doing in there. He only wanted to pay you a thousand, hut I told him we went to school together, and I wouldn't settle for a cent less than *two* thousand, because I knew it would be worth that to him."

"How'd he know about me?" Orvis asked.

"He didn't!" Billy said disgustedly. "*I* knew about you. *You are the only guy I could trust* with such an important mission."

"I'll do it," Orvis had exclaimed, his face glowing with pride that his friend had such trust in him.

"Only you *must* keep it secret," Billy had cautioned. "Don't even let Mary know about it."

Orvis nodded. Intrigue. Espionage. These had been only words to him. Way above his humdrum life as ditch digger for the Acme Plumbing Company. But now they were real.

He had signed the application blank and given it back to Billy, and Billy had mailed it.

Now he was going through the door and sitting down in a chair with a writing arm on it like they used to have in the study hall at high school.

Billy had told him to remember all the questions and tell him what they were. He hoped fervently that they wouldn't be too technical for him to remember.

A SKINNY, stoop-shouldered old guy with a vest and no coat passed up and down the aisles of chairs handing out question sheets. He slapped one down before Orvis and went on, leaving a faint, lingering odor of stale bread.

Orvis looked at the small, black type.

The top line said:

"What would you do? Place a check in the square opposite the thing you would do in the following situations:"

He read over a few of the examples, and confidence returned. This would be easy. He couldn't go wrong. They weren't asking questions where you might give a wrong answer. Why, you could even put down something you *wouldn't* do and they couldn't prove it was the wrong answer.

The first question read:

"You are alone on a beach, and someone in the water is drowning. You can't swim a stroke. There are no boats or other devices that you can use to keep afloat to rescue the drowning person. (1) I would let the person drown. (2) I would go out to save the person.

Orvis thought for a minute, then put an X after the second choice. The second question looked simpler.

It read:

A boat out in a lake is sinking. You row out to rescue the people on it. There are four people on it—two men and two women. None of them can swim, and neither can you. You can take only three people back with you, and the boat will sink before you can return for the fourth. (1) I would take the two women and one of the men. (2) I would take the two men and the younger of the two women.

Orvis put a check after the first alternative. The next situation made him frown. It read:

"An apartment house is burning. Several dozen people are trapped on the roof. From the window of your apartment you toss a rope across to the roof of the burning building, where it is made fast to a chimney. You tie your end to a radiator. The people are panic-stricken and start coming along the rope in a dense string, one right next to the other. You shout that the rope will not support more than three at a time, but they pay no attention to you. You have a loaded rifle in your room, and are absolutely certain that if more than three get on the line—the line will break and they will all be killed, and the rest, on the roof will die in the fire. There are now five on the rope, coming across, and another trying to get on the rope. (1) I would shoot the two last ones on the rope and any more that got on it until the first three reached safety. (2) Shooting any of them would be murder, based on my guess that the line would only hold three. I would let them keep coming, hoping the rope wouldn't break. If it broke, I would not be responsible.

Orvis frowned. There was more here than met the eye. Why should they ask such foolish questions as these just to pick out a few laborers? Which would he actually do, now that the question had been posed? He tried to visualize the scene in his mind. If he shot any of them he would be liable for murder, and his only defense would be that he thought the line wouldn't hold more than three. If he let them keep coming, the line would break. Then he wouldn't be liable under the law for murder, but ALL the people would die. If he shot, he might only have to kill three or four before the rest got some sense in their heads. But you hang just as surely for killing one as a dozen, so the number he would have to kill didn't make any difference.

Another thought came to his mind. Maybe it was a trick question, a trap to make him admit he might kill somebody as the solution to a problem. If you would kill once you would kill again. That's why they hung people.

"I'll play it safe," he muttered to himself. "I won't answer it. If I don't get the job, at least they haven't got anything on me."

The questions took him two hours to answer. There were twenty-five of them, all told. And each pictured a situation where you would have to do something, and no matter what you did, somebody got it in the neck.

When he finished, the man in the vest told him that would be all. He would be notified by mail if he got the job. Billy was waiting for him in his car, and the two went out to a place on the north side where they had high-backed booths and the waitresses left you alone.

There Orvis repeated word for word the whole list of statements and his answers, while Billy wrote them down.

When the list was finished Billy looked it over, more puzzled than Orvis had been.

"What a list of sappy questions," he commented. "But I think you'll get the job. This is just a smoke screen and it doesn't mean anything. And remember, if they make you promise not to say anything about your work to anybody, go ahead and promise. That's what our big spies in foreign countries have to do. Anything goes in war, and this is a war for the freedom of the press…"

Billy's next statement proved that he was a born psychologist. His face became grave and stern. His voice vibrated with emotion as he said:

"Orvis, we are all depending on you. The future of the whole country may depend on you. It is up to you whether we have a dictatorship, or whether we keep the democracy we fought for in two world wars. Don't let us down."

CHAPTER FIVE

CATHERINE stood resting one black-gloved hand on the iron railing that separated the sidewalk from the airfield. The rows of lights that surrounded it cast a spotted curtain of gray shadow across the field with its concrete runs and black earth in between.

At her back was the depot and its banks of floodlights, which made the surrounding area bright as day—to blend in with the lesser light of the field.

In the black, overcast sky, lights were drifting slowly downward, connected by some invisible structure that held them together, blinking monotonously their red, green, and white colors.

The lights spread slowly apart as they lowered, until at last they came to earth at the far end of the field. At the same time the huge bulk of the four-engined transcontinental plane materialized, reflected the field lights from its aluminum skin.

The throaty roar of its motors burst forth as it picked up speed across the runway. At the last moment it performed a quarter turn, pivoting on one giant wheel, and with a final snort stood docile and silent.

Catherine stood on her toes and craned her neck, peering intently at the windows of the plane, hoping to catch a glimpse of her father and Jerry; but all she could see was the midsections of people, men and women, as they stood in the aisle ready to disembark.

A uniformed attendant was wheeling a set of steps to the plane. The door of the plane came part way open and the head of the stewardess appeared for a moment. Then the door opened wide and people started descending to the pavement.

Alex appeared, followed immediately by, Jerry. Catherine waved one arm, steadying her body with the other gripping the rail. Jerry had seen her and was waving back. Then they were blocked out by the people ahead of them as they came down the fence-lined walk, like cattle to the slaughter in a stockyard.

Catherine waited impatiently, smiling and waving each time the head of Alex or Jerry bobbed into view. At last Alex emerged and she threw her arms around him for a moment, then delicately kissed Jerry on the lips.

She flooded the two with questions that she gave them no time to answer, all the way through the depot out to the car.

Olly looked up as they came, and then opened the door and climbed out, holding himself erect with his right hand on the top of the car door, a broad grin of welcome on his face.

As the red Buick backed out from the curb and moved forward into the night, a dark green sedan followed discreetly. Behind the dark windshield were two men, one driving, and the other with a pair of headphones clamped to his ears.

In the back seat a standard record player was running, its cutting needle peeling fine threads from a light-colored blank.

"What did you do in Washington?" the voice of Catherine came faintly, along with the hum of the motor.

"Nothing much," Alex's voice replied. "And all that we did do must be kept secret, so don't keep asking us about it."

The voices became indistinct, so the man with the headphones leaned over the seat and twisted a knob on the record player. The motor noises came louder, but through them Catherine's voice could be heard.

"Did you miss me, Jerry?" she was saying.

"I thought about you a great deal," Jerry answered.

"He was the most love sick person I ever saw," Alex contributed with a chuckle. "It was sickening just to watch him."

"That wasn't lovesickness, that was—" Jerry stopped abruptly.

"What?" Catherine's voice came, tantalizing.

"Something I ate that didn't agree with me," Jerry said hastily. "Some corned beef hash."

There was silence for awhile up ahead.

"This gadget works pretty good, doesn't it," the driver of the green sedan said to the man with the headphones.

"Yeah," was the answer. Johnny was right. "They haven't said anything, but the girl will worm it out of her boy friend as soon as they are alone somewhere. Wait and see. All we've got to do is see that they never get out of earshot of the recorder, and we'll get all the evidence we need."

"What about the transmitter in their car?" the driver sounded worried. "Think they'll discover it? If they do the g-men will be on our tails quick."

"Not a chance. That radio friend of mine worked on it all one night getting it in place. The box is fastened inside the crossbeams of the frame, where no one could ever see it, and the mike is in the upholstering where it will never be found. The switch is in the seat. One of those long affairs so that any pressure anywhere on the seat closes it. The whole thing runs off the car battery and is tied up so that it doesn't show on the amp meter. It can stay where it is, and won't be found until the car is dismantled for junk."

"What about the house?" the driver asked.

"We've got mikes all over the place. And in Chadwick's apartment, too. None of them can say a word without it going down on a recording. Even what they say in their sleep will be recorded."

"That will take a lot of records, won't it?"

"No, we just let them run, and if nothing is said we just cut them over again."

JERRY set his suitcase on the sidewalk and opened the sidewalk door to the stairs that led to their apartment, holding it open until Olly was inside. Then, picking up his suitcase he followed Olly's dragging figure up the stairs. He had dropped Alex and Catherine at their house and not stayed.

Upstairs, Olly said:

"Well, it's nice to have you back home again, Jerry." Then, putting his finger to his lips, he handed Jerry a sheet of paper.

On it Olly had typed:

"Be careful what you say. Somebody has put small listening devices all over the place. I discovered them two days ago."

"It's good to be back, Olly," Jerry replied. "How's your book coming?"

"Let's go down to the corner and have a coke or something," Olly suggested.

"Yeah," Jerry agreed." I don't feel like turning in yet."

They went down to the street again and walked three-quarters of a block to Marty's Hamburger Shop. No one was there except the white-aproned waiter and cook.

Olly sat down in one of the booths; Jerry ordered two hamburgers and coffees and put several nickels in the jukebox. When the strains of *Cool Water,* as sung by the Sons of the Pioneers, began, drowning out any other sounds within a few feet, Olly began explaining rapidly.

"A newspaper reporter called on me. He said his paper wanted to run a story about me and my work in their Sunday paper, and wanted a picture to go with it," he said. "The reporter took me down to the paper and had their photographer take several shots of me. When I got home I noticed that the easy chair had been moved slightly from where it always sets. I knew it had been moved. So I started looking around carefully. I found three black mikes of the button type, with fine wires leading outside. I didn't follow them up because I didn't know what I'd run into. There's one on the stairs and in the lab, too."

"Hmm," Jerry said thoughtfully." I don't know what it's all about, but we'd better let somebody know about this."

"Another thing," Olly said. "You know that letter you sent me from Washington? It had been steamed open, and I got it a day later than the postman left it. When I saw it had been steamed open I asked the mailman when he had left it. He said Wednesday, and I didn't get it until Thursday!"

There was a phone booth against the back wall of the cafe. Jerry had the waiter change two paper dollars for him, and then went into the booth.

"I want to send a telegram to Washington, D.C.," he said when he got the telegraph office. Then, after a pause, "To Washington, D.C., five-five-oh. The message is, 'Need help on microphone hookup. Setup wrong when I arrived.'"

After that he went back and sat down opposite Olly in the booth.

"We'll just ignore the mikes until we hear from the ones I just sent the telegram to," he said to Olly. "We don't need to worry so long as we don't talk about what I did in Washington, and we won't talk about that anyway."

"What's it all about?" Olly asked curiously. "You should be able to tell me about it. I'm your brother."

"All I'll say is that I wish to God I didn't know about it myself," Jerry exclaimed. "No matter what happens, don't even try to find out."

"Okay," Olly gave in. "Would you like to hear what I've been doing since you left?"

AT JERRY'S nod he began, eagerly. "Life took two different courses from the initial, methyl alcohol stage at the beginning. Analyzing it from the laboratory data I have so far, I would say that from the very start, almost, it switched to the hydrocarbon molecule, too, so that the hydrocarbon and the hydroxicarbon forms developed. Their evolution should be easy to discover, up to the time the hydroxicarbon evolution developed the cell sac. The hydrocarbon couldn't produce a cell wall to protect it from environment, so it never got any farther than the petroleum stage. That is probably the source of our oil deposits—hydrocarbon life multiplying and seeping into the earth. It gravitated toward pockets where it stayed. The hydroxicarbons, with their oxygen atoms on them, finally developed to the point where they produced cellulose, which formed fine films around the reproducing substance. From then on, in the protection of the cell wall, more and more complex molecules were possible."

"What caused the changes in the molecules as they kept on building up and breaking off, or reproducing?" asked Jerry.

"That probably was very common in the beginning," Olly said. "For each molecule that could reproduce, there were many different reactions possible that produced new molecular types. Some of these were life types also, and multiplied. After the first few changes, types were produced that couldn't possibly have resulted directly from natural chemical synthesis in non-living substances. And the Earth was getting cooler and cooler all the time, too. This cooling made more complex types possible, and probably ended the production of the petroleum types. Today, in the cracking process, where we make high-octane gas, we have to put a little high octane in the petroleum vapor to start the process. The life principle in operation."

"And to think," Jerry exclaimed, "that for all the untold centuries since man could tell the difference between living and non-living things he thought that life was due to some special *elan* that animated matter!"

"Yes," Olly said, a new note of gravity in his voice. "I wonder how mankind is going to take it? The proof that life is a perfectly chemical process will poke holes in most of the existing theories about the nature of man's soul, since they rest on the 'unknowableness' of the fundamental nature of life. To me, at least, it doesn't refute the existence of the soul, because you and I, being trained in science, have always felt that if man is immortal, there must be a material and perfectly normal vehicle of existence for his soul."

"That's right," Jerry agreed soberly. "To the man of the street, I suppose, matter with its atoms and molecules, making up bricks, dirt, oceans and all material objects, seems like something too common for construction of the immortal soul of a man. To the scientist, who sees in the atom something finer and more intricate than the finest watch, who sees in the workings of the universe something more majestic and Godlike than the untrained mind can even begin to appreciate, it is something else. I don't know how to express it."

"I know," Olly answered, his fine, intellectual face lighting up at the vision his mind could encompass but hardly put into words. "One might as well try to give the uneducated man a word picture of the beauty of a mathematical structure as to try to put into words what a beautiful thing the universe is in its basic structure."

"Well," Jerry said with a sudden smile, "we might as well go home and get some shut-eye. Do you realize it's almost two A.M.?"

JERRY was not able to sleep. He lay awake and thought. And by one of those inexplicable coincidences that must occur quite often, since they are accidentally uncovered from time to time and must certainly go undetected most of the time—across the continent to the east the President was perfecting a plan which would permit the building of the caves as a security measure against attack. And in Chicago a group of engineers were putting the finishing touches on the plans for a tunnel borer which could carve an eight-foot bore through solid rock at the rate of two feet an hour.

In England the house of Lords was gradually bringing order out of chaos in its mad heterogeny of plans, all of which recognized the futility of boring underground in the British Isles.

And in Russia the Supreme Soviet was finally realizing that plans and ambitions they had nursed from their first beginnings were now meaningless. As one of them put it so aptly:

"Of what use is it for men to fight for the command of a sinking ship?"

The reasoning, capitalism and communism can't exist side by side, therefore one of them must go, had been met in an unexpected manner by Fate with her answer, therefore both of them must go."

At the same instant that Jerry, having decided that it might be possible that the race could be perpetuated underground, and that if this were so it was quite probable that he would be among those whose offspring would be saved so that there was no immediate reason for him to break off with Catherine turned over with a relieved sigh and went to sleep, the President was outlining the bold strokes of his great plan.

"First," he typed, "the cavern cities can't be started openly unless a proper excuse for them is given to the public. The only reason they might accept is one based on the threat of impending war. A war in which the adversary also has atom bombs."

"Therefore," he concluded, "Russia must do something to make this threat seem real."

He outlined tentative things Russia might do. She might resign from the United Nations. On top of this she might hold an atom bomb experiment of her own someplace. Things calculated to make the public believe war was a certainty, and that caverns would be the only protection from atom bomb attacks.

Meanwhile the governments of all countries could carry on the work of carving our long tunnels far under the surface, and huge cavern cities a mile or so down, in solid, unbroken granite.

While in Russia the President had made plans for the installation of direct, wired television with Stalin on special frequencies. This installation had been in for two days now.

It took only a few minutes for the President to contact the Russian Premier. Stalin agreed that the plan was not only feasible, but perhaps the *only* feasible plan. For several hours the details of the plan were discussed. The great danger of the plan would be that some incident might touch off public opinion in either country and precipitate an actual war. They both agreed that if they themselves each announced often and emphatically that the other would have to make the first definite, hostile attack before they would agree to an actual war, that peace could be maintained.

CHAPTER SIX

IT WAS a peculiar state of affairs that existed during the winter of 1947-48. In all past history the common people of inimical countries had not wanted war. It had been the leaders who worked up the war spirit to the point where the common man felt he had to fight—for patriotism, to preserve his freedom, to get the other fellow before he got you, or to rescue some 'friendly' nation that you conveniently forgot had been knifing you in the back before he was attacked.

If the fate of the world had not been irrevocably fixed by unforeseen circumstances, indications were that Russia would have resigned from the United Nations and declared a Monroe Doctrine for Europe, and after that for Eurasia, and precipitated another world conflict. And that the English-speaking world would have welcomed it in the hope that the threat of communism would be ended by that war.

If Alex Topanov had not figured out the last, awful consequences of the simple explosions of five atom bombs, perhaps that is the way history would have run. Then the nations would have awoke to the fate of humanity with its time shortened by a full century, and mankind would have gone down to utter extinction.

But during that winter the people of the world cried for war, and the leaders held them back with the stall, "Let the others cast the first stone so that our victory will be justified in history." Only instead of a stone it would be an atom bomb.

In October Russia resigned from the United Nations. The papers predicted war within twenty-four hours with daily regularity. Toward the end of October the British Government moved to Canada, and an evacuation of the British Isles began, which lasted throughout the winter, until there were less than fifteen million people left in all the British Isles. They went to

Canada in passenger liners and freight boats. They had private staterooms and they had floor space in the hold of the ship. After the Russian atom bomb experiment, the Britishers came over densely packed, fasting until they reached America because there wasn't room to carry food on the ships that brought them.

The government leaders and scientists of the world, knowing the secret reasons for the migration, prayed that no ship would meet with disaster. If just one of the ships sank it could mean the overthrow of a government and open war. For it had been decided that open war was preferable to revealing the secret and loosing a panic upon the world that would probably defeat the plans to save humanity from extinction. Fortunately, not one ship met with disaster in the "migration," as it became known.

Thousands died after reaching Canada, from malnutrition, exposure caused by the impossibility of finding shelter for nine-tenths of the population of the British Isles in the bleak winterlands of southern Canada, and disease contracted on the ships in spite of all precautions.

For the emergency both the United States and Great Britain moved all available ships into the Great Lakes, where they were anchored off the Canadian beaches. These housed over two million of the migrants. Other millions were sheltered in flimsy Quonset huts, storerooms, and even tents.

There were almost daily tragedies. On Christmas day a huge circus tent housing five thousand women and children caught fire fatally, burning over eight hundred of the women, and sending almost a thousand to the hospitals with serious burns. The migrants living in the hospitals had to move out almost en masse, with no place to go. Many of them died of exposure.

ON THE surface there was the greatest war hysteria ever known. Underneath, the leaders and technicians who knew what was going on moved quietly and in harmony. Before the spring of 1947 they had grown used to the certainty that their every decision meant loss of life and property. Such consequences were inescapable.

But, just as a mass of U-235 rests quietly in its container until it reaches a critical mass, then in a few awful seconds unleashes its titanic energies to throw cubic miles of water into the heavens and send seismic waves, through the earth, to cause earthquakes months later in the nodal areas of the waves, so also the state of affairs in the world of men, as it was during that winter, gradually reached the critical mass, or stage of complexity and development, where it could be touched off by adding just a little more. Hindsight is always infallible. By the summer of 1948 the world leaders could see that what took place was inevitable. But in the fall of 1947 it seemed only possible but not probable.

Certainly it was only a remote possibility on that morning in September when Jerry's telegram to the Secret Service, informing them of the planted microphones in the apartment, was laid on the President's desk. It lay there for half an hour while the President continued his discussion with Stalin of the pros and cons of the plan to use war hysteria as the motivating force for building of underground cities, all interconnected, deep in the bedrock of the Earth.

Two hours later, however, a jet plane took off from a field near Washington, D.C., and sped across the country; and in the course of time one of the several young men in the secret service that Jerry and Alex would know by sight knocked on the door to Jerry's apartment.

Jerry recognized him at once, and guessed he had come because of the telegram.

"Hello, Hugh," Jerry exclaimed. "Come on up. My brother, Olly, is out right now, so we'll have the place all to ourselves." He turned and led the way up the stairs, pointing silently to the small mike placed inconspicuously above a strip of molding near the ceiling of the stair well.

The young man, Hugh Montague, nodded grimly. In the apartment the two carried on a casual exchange of patter while Jerry pointed out the other mikes, and the fine wires leading to the outside.

Finally Hugh handed Jerry a typewritten sheet which read:

"From now on, ostensibly, we are threatened by war, and all our actions and discussions will be based on the theory that we must hasten defenses against an aggressive war by Russia.

"Therefore you are at liberty to divulge to your brother in this apartment that the purpose of your visit to the Capital was for the purpose of cooperating in the design of atomic power to drive boring machines which will be used to construct atom proof shelters beneath all the major cities, with connecting bores so that any catastrophe in one section can be dealt with without exposing our defenses to attack.

"In line with this plan you will shortly receive an appointment actually to participate in the perfection of atom motor design at Hanford, Washington. Dr. Topanov will remain at the University and carry on studies aimed at nullifying, if possible, the eventual effects of that with which we were concerned in our recent discussions.

"No further mention will be made of the Topanov-Chadwick Report except in the protection of the Capital. All activities directly connected with that report will also remain secret. If at any time it becomes necessary to discuss some phase of the report, use the code word, *aeroplane,* with that spelling.

"Discuss the fictitious reason for your trip to Washington with your brother with great reluctance, for the benefit of those on the other end of the listening devices. Don't be alarmed, as we will be very careful not to let anything happen to you."

It was signed by the President.

When Jerry had finished reading it, Hugh crumpled it up and placed it in an ashtray, setting fire to it. Both men watched until it was nothing but embers. Then Hugh poked at it until there was nothing left except fine ashes.

JOHNNY DAVIS sat in his office, alone, and with his feet resting on the glass surface of his desk. Fresh in his mind was all the latest data on the present events. He was sorting and analyzing it.

Highest on the list in importance was the half-dozen records flown from Seattle, giving the conversation between Jerry Chadwick and his brother, Olliver Chadwick.

It revealed that there was secret government information, as yet unknown, which indicated that Russia was making atom bombs. The danger seemed so great that the United States and the British governments were making hasty efforts to build bomb proof shelters under all large cities by perfecting a huge, automatic boring machine, powered by atom motors.

Chadwick was awaiting orders to go to Hanford to work on the motors. Topanov was to remain at the university and make further experiments with the theoretical aspects of the source of atomic power.

A lucky break had enabled a reporter in Chicago to find out that an experimental model of the boring machine was being built. It was being rushed, and there were more technicians on the job than workmen.

From England Johnny had a report that there was an extraordinary convening of the Parliament, and that reporters were barred. This by itself did not mean anything in particular, but coupled with all the other information it could mean a lot—especially since it had been going on for two weeks now, with no sign of the members getting ready to go back home.

One collection of items puzzled Johnny. It appeared that hundreds of freighters in Pacific ports and graveyards of the inland waters of the Pacific coast were being hastily manned and moved through Panama to the East Coast. Most surprising of all was the fact that three out of four of the crews were Canadian, from the captain on down. The ships carried only ballast, and the crews knew nothing except that they were being paid almost twice the union scale.

These empty ships were moving through the Panama Canal at the rate of ten a day. Some of them were ships on regular runs, which dumped their cargoes in California, Oregon, or Washington, and then went to the canal instead of back to South America.

The reporter to replace George Cramil in Moscow had reached Russia, and should be starting his secret report in a few days.

As yet, Orvis Oshiboski (Johnny smiled every time he thought of the name) had not been hired for the Hanford job. If and when he was, he would serve as a check on information from other sources.

All in all, Johnny felt that something really big was underway, but there was not enough to go on. News on other fronts was plentiful.

The strike situation was getting worse daily. Congress was debating legislation to relieve the meat shortage, and getting nowhere. A bill had been introduced that would make farmers register all livestock, with stiff penalties for violations. Then the farmers would be told when to market their stock.

Meat rationing would probably be back by the end of the year, with registering of meat in private cold storage boxes, and stiff penalties for violation.

Confidential reports indicated that several large companies were building plants in South America to get around labor problems. One of the nation's leading industrial magnates was rumored to have applied for Bolivian citizenship, although there was no verification of this rumor.

Johnny took his feet off his desk and pulled out the typewriter and began to type out his news program for the day. At the top of the sheet he wrote the date, October 1st.

ON OCTOBER second, Russia resigned from the United Nations. Molotov was not present. An unimportant aide read off the letter of resignation of his government. It began with the word, whereas, which was followed by two thousand words listing all the grievances against the setup and actions of the United Nations. Then followed a statement setting forth Russia's policy for the near future. There were two main sections. The first stated plainly that Russia would wage no War of aggression. The second stated plainly that Russia would use troops to oust British and American troops from any European or Asiatic country.

The document was explicit and complete. Within a certain area of the world, definitely described, Russia declared a Monroe Doctrine. But in addition she declared that no matter what the grievance, she would not send troops outside this area, either for defense or aggression. Furthermore, she would make no military pacts either for mutual defense or attack with any nation outside this area, nor would she honor any such pact made by any nation within her announced sphere of domination.

For two days the papers carried nothing but this news on their front pages. Murders, strikes, and politics went to the inside pages.

But not even Johnny Davis, the scoop-hound, suspected that the President of the United States was the author of the first draft of this Russian Monroe Doctrine and much of its final wording, and that it had been approved by a secret Congressional committee, and also by a similar special committee of the British House of Lords before being handed over to the United Nations group.

The secret wires from the Kremlin and the White House and Buckingham Palace were hot practically twenty-four hours a day as discussions of every phase of the world problems went on. Not every nation was in on it. Some nations had governments too unstable or leaders too temporary to trust them with such a serious responsibility.

On October third, the President spoke to the nation over the radio. In his speech he said he believed Russia when she declared she would not attack outside her sphere of domination. And he reiterated the nation's time-honored policy of not attacking until attacked, and said that since Russia had explicitly marked her sphere, so long as she did not violate her own word it would be respected by the United States.

Attacks began against the President's speech almost before he finished it. The Senator So-and-so who was a special friend of Johnny Davis cried out that it was tossing beloved France to the wolves—or in this case the bear. Cries of appeasement went up on every hand. The almost impossible labor situation was pointed out as evidence of the incompetence of the President, and coupled with his policy toward Russia gave the senator a pliant audience for his cries for impeachment.

On the evening of October fifth, senator So-and-so made an impassioned speech in which he demanded the country impeach the President and hold a special election for a short term President who would use the atom club that the U.S. alone held to beat Russia to her knees and rescue France and Poland from the slavery of communism.

Two hours after he finished, when the special editions of the daily papers were hitting the streets with his speech printed in full on the front page, Stalin impassively announced at a special news conference that Russia would hold her own atom bomb experiment. The news stunned the English-speaking world.

The entire, verbatim interview went over the radio in half an hour, to be followed an hour or two later by further extras on the streets. It went as follows:

Moscow, October 5, 1946: —(U.P.) Oscar Janas, U.P. correspondent. With no advance warning Premier Stalin called a news conference today. Half an hour after I first learned of it and was whisked, almost without ceremony, to the building where the conference was to be held, Stalin appeared with a staff of interpreters and made his announcement, reading from a prepared paper. The text of this paper is as follows:

On Tuesday, October fifteenth, an atom bomb will be exploded in a wasteland in Siberia, far from human habitation. This explosion will not be a repetition of the experiments conducted by the United States, but will be to determine the effectiveness of the atom bomb for defense.

Due to special construction of the bomb, it is hoped that the blast will expend itself in a horizontal direction. The bomb will be fired from a specially constructed gun on the ground and will be set to explode at a height of twenty thousand feet.

There will be two-hundred robot-controlled dummy planes flying at various distances and heights from the blast and also instruments on the ground directly under the blast and for many miles in all directions from it, to measure the concussion that reaches the ground, and also the extent of radiation and its intensity. In addition there will be many specially constructed cameras to record the blast.

The object of this experiment is to determine whether the atom bomb can be used effectively, with relatively little danger to life on the surface, to repel an attack by air. The success of the experiment will depend on the construction of the bomb, and will be a success or failure, depending on whether the design confines the blast principally to a thin, horizontal plane, or fails in its purpose and permits the blast to reach the ground.

Due to a new type of neutron reflector the bomb will not need to be as large as those used by the United States. The new reflector reduces the critical mass almost half.

Observers from the United States and Britain are being invited to observe the effects of the explosion, just as we were invited to observe the Bikini experiments.

There was a stunned silence after Stalin had finished his calm reading of the paper. Finally a British reporter got back his voice.

"Then Russia now has the secret of the atom bomb and her own plants for manufacturing them?" he asked.

"Of course," Stalin replied. "And we also have the world's largest deposits of pitchblende. Our geologists estimate that we have over two million pounds of uranium accessible for atomic power within the borders of the Soviet Union."

By this time I had regained my own voice. I asked:

"Do you have, or are you making bombs of the type used at Bikini?"

Stalin smiled and ignored my question. But from his smile I gathered that Russia has bombs on hand. Whether this is so, or if Russia has just been able to gather the materials for the one bomb, and is staging a gigantic bluff in an attempt to back up her recently-declared Monroe Doctrine for Europe, is anyone's guess.

Seattle, Wa., October 5, (U.P.) Dr. Topanov, world's greatest atom scientist, today said that Russia probably is not bluffing. His statement is as follows: "In my opinion, the Soviet Union is in a better position to wage atom warfare than any other country in the world. Her population is for the most part decentralized. Two bombs, one dropped on Chicago and the other on New York, could wipe out a good percentage of the population of the United States. No two bombs dropped anywhere in Russia could wipe out more than a small fraction of one percent of its population.

"It is well known," Dr. Topanov continued, "that Russia contains considerably more than half the world's known heavy metal deposits. In addition, she has the know-how in industrial technique. If she now knows how to manufacture the materials that make the atom bomb, and has plants like ours at Hanford and other places, she can catch up to us in atom achievement if she has not done so already."

THIS was followed by a bitter statement from Senator So-and-so in which he said that if the President had taken his advice we could have brought Russia to her knees before she had a chance to get atom bombs. This seemed a trifle illogical since the senator's advice had been given just two hours before the Soviet announcement.

No one knew of the B29 that had taken the bomb Russia was to use for the experiment from the United States to Siberia. No one knew that the men who would direct the experiment were officers in the United States Army. They were men of the growing group who knew the secret of the world's coming doom, and therefore could be trusted to keep their secret.

Not all who were let in on the secret could be trusted, in spite of the precautions taken to find out the beliefs and integrity of the men beforehand. But all were closely watched, in secret, and many met with "accidents" just before they could let the secret out.

On October fourteenth, the first boring machine bent its nose downward a mile south of the southern tip of Lake Michigan. It ploughed easily through the soft stone that underlies the dirt in the basin around the lake. The engineers pronounced the trial a success.

Announcement of the success of the boring machine quieted somewhat the panic created by the worry over what Russia would do with the atom bomb. In fact, many people were sneering disdainfully as the hour for the Russian experiment neared, and saying:

"Let them have the atom bomb. We've got protection against it now."

Others pointed out that having a machine to carve out protection against bombs, and having the protection, were two different things. That Russia, if she had the bombs, might strike at once before bomb shelters could be built.

Still others pointed out hopefully, yet ludicrously, that perhaps the Russian bomb would disrupt the substructures of Siberia and cause it to sink beneath the ocean level, thus reducing the size and population of Russia to such an extent that it wouldn't be a threat to the world.

THE morning sun of October fifteenth crept up over a bleak horizon in the northern wasteland where the bomb was resting in the maw of a huge cannon.

The white landscape was cut by a lone file of wooden poles that led from the black area of the cannon and buildings to the horizon on the west. It was over this wire that the signal would be sent that would start the bomb on its journey into the stratosphere.

Here and there over the landscape were smaller dark spots where cameras and other equipment were placed. Invisible, though still an important part of the ground equipment, were the various wild animals in the area.

The sun had just shaken off the last, clinging tendril of horizon and paused briefly before beginning its upward climb, when the droning of many planes came from the southward hills.

Far up in the clear sky dots emerged, widely distributed. The foremost ones passed overhead and kept on toward the north, until at last the sky was evenly dotted from horizon to horizon with widely spaced planes.

A puff of smoke rose from the mouth of the huge cannon and a silver streak climbed rapidly into the heavens. Before the sound of the cannon blast could travel a mile a sun came into being in the stratosphere, growing with unbelievable speed so that it spread over the heavens faster than the eye could measure.

The huge sun changed from flaming heat to calm, white quiescence; and through the newly born clouds drifted crippled planes, to plough their noses into the white snow below.

The snow itself, which had been sharp and crystalline, took on a glistening, glassy appearance after awhile; and after the last plane had fallen, and the crash of its fall had echoed and re-echoed into oblivion, silence crept cautiously back from the distant places and sat uneasily on its disturbed throne.

Only the faint, almost inaudible clicking sounds from the instruments as they sent their messages over the wires that hung from the poles, disturbed the blanket of quiet.

At the other end of that solitary line of poles, miles away, activity was intense. Men in the uniforms of the Red and the United States Army dashed from teletype machines to plotting boards. And out of their activity was arising a complete picture of the explosion.

It had been a success. A complete success. But there were several peculiar and unpredicted effects. For one, the atmospheric pressure as recorded by the instruments on the ground had rapidly dropped from normal to almost nothing during the explosion, rising slowly back to normal.

Beginning about three miles from the center of the blast a pressure wave had traveled along the surface. This wave, beginning almost imperceptibly, increased in amplitude for a mile, indicating that it was fed from the upper atmosphere, then decreased with the inverse square law. It traveled fifty feet faster per second than sound and was about half a mile thick.

The explosion itself concentrated its blast in a plane about two thousand feet thick and spread out on a radius of nearly seven miles, collapsing and buckling the parts of all planes in a two hundred square mile area.

Radio operators were busy transmitting the data as quickly as it became available, so that in every major city in the world the man on the street knew almost as much as the men on the spot.

The man on the street was jubilant. The defense against the atom bomb was the atom bomb! The few thousands who knew of the insidious cancer that would destroy life in three more centuries were regretful and sad, for they knew that the experiment would shorten that time by a few years, and that a major atomic war might cut it to less than a century.

ON OCTOBER twentieth, the British government announced to the world its intention to desert the British Isles. On the same day the first twenty ships left England with their human cargoes for Canada.

Russia was silent. The President of the United States made a statement to the effect that his government would aid in the migration in every way possible. His use of the word, migration, hit the public fancy, and from that time on the exodus became know as "the migration," and each one who came over during that period became tagged for the rest of his life as a migrant.

Several writers from the United States went to England and came over with the migrants to gather material for books, which became immediate best sellers.

CHAPTER SEVEN

DURING October and November the seething volcano of public unrest began to grow. Senator So-and-so, emboldened by the favorable reaction to his speech against the President, began a systematic campaign, with material supplied by Johnny Davis which he dared not use himself because of lack of evidence, which did much to stir the masses.

He could, and did, say that from an unimpeachable source he had definite assurance that the President had visited Moscow secretly. Called before a Senate Committee he refused to divulge the source of his information, simply repeating:

"Let the President appear on this floor under oath and deny that he made such a trip. Then I will retract my statement publicly."

The President's answer to this was:

"It would be silly for me to treat seriously the rantings of the senator and play into his insane campaign of heckling to the extent of appearing on the floor of the Senate to state for his benefit something which should be obvious to anyone with common sense."

Senator So-and-so visited the various labor leaders, making sure that the newspapers played up these visits. Immediately after, new union tactics came into play. In Chicago a strike brought into play one of these new tactics. Butchers were forbidden during a strike of an entirely unrelated group to sell meat, what there was of it, to anyone who could not produce a union membership card.

By the end of November every union member in the country had one of the new "fight" cards. They were wallet-sized. It was threatened that by the spring of forty-seven no one could buy anything without one of these cards.

Organizing campaigns were speeded up. The threat of the fighting card produced results. Farmers were organized under a union. Small business owners also had to join. The motto of the unions became, "everyone in a union by May, forty-seven."

In spite of the threat of the fighting card, large groups held out, and very few farmers joined. One large farm group that had been in existence for many years openly defied the unions.

The union answer was to call strikes in all farm machinery factories, and prohibit sales to farmers without fighting cards after May first, 1948—several months away.

The President stepped in and ordered the workers in the strikebound farm machinery plants back to work. Riots resulted, and the President sent in troops to impose his demands.

The Christmas Riots, as they became known, were the beginning of the open rift between government and labor. G.I.s, who were disgusted with the housing shortage and the continual strikes, went back into the army.

Accusations were tossed about indiscriminately. The housing shortage was due to governmental stupidity, to shirking of the construction workers, to strikes, to everything that could be remotely connected with it.

Real estate prices shot up so that a house that had been priced at five thousand in 1930, and at fifteen thousand in the fall of 1946, was priced at fifty thousand dollars by the first of January, 1948. No house could be rented.

The idea of the cooperative apartment house spread, so that by December, 1947, many apartment house owners were selling their apartment houses by apartments. A good example of this was the owner of a north Chicago, twenty-apartment building, who gave notice of eviction to all his tenants and offered his apartments for sale at thirty thousand each. Records showed that he had bought the building for twenty-five thousand dollars in 1935.

Christmas toys of the same identical design and construction which had sold for less than a dollar in 1935 sold for as high as twenty-five dollars in December, 1947.

The man on the street in that same month was wearing a sport shirt, doubtfully sanforized, price fifty dollars, a summer weight sport coat, price seventy-five dollars, a pair of sport slacks, price sixty dollars, and a pair of perforated sport shoes, price twenty-five dollars. Suits were selling for three hundred dollars. Dress shirts, dress shoes, and most other items of wearing apparel were not to be had.

The sensible person who bought any article of clothing had it entirely resewed before wearing it. The resewing cost an additional four dollars for a sport shirt, which itself cost fifty dollars and was made of cotton or rayon.

Turkeys that sold for eighty cents a pound for Thanksgiving, shot up to a dollar thirty-five a pound for Christmas.

Unions struck for a living wage for the worker, and by the time their demands were granted, the "living" wage they asked for was inadequate.

OSWALD SPENGLER, in his *Decline of the West,* stated that in any system of government there are certain good points and certain weaknesses; and that eventually the weaknesses grow to such proportions that they destroy the system.

A man owns many houses from which he derives a modest income during ordinary times in the form of rents. He can sell these houses for about what he paid for them, but if he does he loses a source of income in rents, so he keeps them.

Suddenly property values shoot up because of the housing shortage. The owner is able to sell for a profit that is greater than several years' income from rents. He sees that in a year or two the housing shortage will probably end, and values drop back to normal, so he *sells*, planning on buying again when values drop. Real estate values grow, until a working man must pay more than he can earn in a normal lifetime for a house in which to live.

A shirt manufacturer has made a fair living supplying all kinds of shirts. The demand exceeds the possible supply, so the government clamps on price ceilings, but leaves them off sport clothes. The manufacturer, caring only for the profit, makes sport shirts, forcing the man on the street to wear sport shirts in the winter and the summer alike.

The butcher, selling his meat on a profit basis, sells a piece of meat to a man for three dollars, knowing that the man cannot afford to pay more than a dollar for it out of what he earns. The profit motive blinds him to human values. If the butcher down the street could sell the same meat, or ANY meat for a reasonable price, *he* would have to sell at a loss or lose all of his investment. The butcher makes sixty cents profit on the three dollars worth of meat, where he sold it for sixty cents and made twelve cents profit in 1935. It is his legitimate profit, on a percentage basis.

The farmer raises beans and plows them under because he can only make six cents profit a pound on them in 1947, where he was glad to *get* six cents a pound for them in 1935. The pressures of monopoly, which in times of plenty could only be used by huge corporations, and against which laws were passed to ensure free competition, became the common weapon of the little man—the man who owned a house he couldn't use, and for which there were ten thousand buyers with money and no place to sleep, the man with ANYTHING, and people without it who need it and can't get it.

Who was to blame? The government? The labor unions? The property owners? The farmers? Or the capitalist system? It really goes down to two incompatible principles that exist side by side in the profit system, eternally in conflict, their warfare balanced in ordinary times, but thrust out of balance by circumstances. These principles are: (1) to make as much profit as possible in any business transaction, and (2) to get as much for your money as possible.

In a stable system the average individual gets as much as he produces in dollars and man-hours. If he gets more than his share it follows that some must get less than their share. If he sells a house and makes a profit that is equivalent to the wages of the average man working for two years, it means that the average man must work two years for nothing to make it up. It is inescapable.

Your answer:

"Should I pass up an opportunity to make a huge profit legitimately just because, in the last analysis SOMEONE must work to earn the profit I made; even though it will never be me?"

Who knows? And what difference will it make in three hundred years? Hitler said that the weakness of a democracy is that no individual is responsible for anything. You feel justified in depriving the average man of the fruits of two years' labor for the sake of your individual profit on a deal because you are not responsible for the welfare of anyone except yourself and your immediate family.

The average man demands through his union an exorbitant return for his labor because he is not responsible for the welfare of the owner who wants to make a profit on his product. He tries to get out of that two years of working for nothing by increased wages. The employer tries to get out of it by raising the price of his product. The buyer tries to get out of it by raising his own prices.

And in the end no one gets out of it. It is simple arithmetic. If you produce a dollar's worth of wealth and get three for it, SOMEONE must produce two dollars' worth for nothing. "But not me!" You hear someone whisper. Maybe not. That is the lure of free enterprise, and its reward. And also its weakness when it gets out of bounds.

THE least to blame is labor, for labor produces most of the wealth and reaps only part of the fruits at any time. But its relative innocence is due not to its purity but its position in the scheme of things. Consisting of the workers, the creators or inventors followed by the actual workers who turn out the products of invention in large volume, whether these are new types of vegetables or a book, a hunting rifle or a washing machine, the laboring class is for the most part a passive pawn in the chess game of national industry and politics.

The laboring class not only produces the wealth, it also buys most of it. But in buying it loses out, for it must support the property owner, who does no work, and the host of stockholders who do no work. In addition it must support the entire framework of government and government works, regardless of all tax-the-rich laws. This is compensated for by the fact that the average worker does more than his necessary share of producing wealth, in normal times. The ratio of the wealth produced to the buying power gained by the average worker determines the stability of the system.

If production of wealth increases, in the form of manufactured products and foodstuffs, while buying power gained decreases, or increases more slowly, the system eventually breaks down. In 1929 credit buying disrupted the system in that way.

If buying power increases while production of wealth drops below normal, inflationary tendencies and monopolistic practices disrupt the system. During the period from 1939 to 1945 production of wealth was by-passed to instruments of warfare, so that buying power increased while available wealth produced declined.

Scarcity created millions of monopolistic corners in markets. The system broke down again. People with lots of money slept in parks and went hungry. A depression in goods instead of buying power set in. The reverse of 1929, but just as evil.

In 1929 a man did not have an electric toaster because he had no money to buy it, so the man who made them lost his job because there was no market.

In 1936 a man did not have an electric toaster because the man who made them could not earn the bare necessities of life by making them, so he struck for a living wage. Why not? Hadn't he saved enough during the war to live on during the strike?

Thus it was. And with the threat of war, the constant attacks on the government, and the final crystallization of power over labor in the hands of a few men, the stability of the economic system went completely overboard. Then it was ripe for self-destruction.

Little things. They are the straws that show which way the great, invisible winds are blowing. The hijacking of a truckload of soap. The condoning of the black market openly in the press as the only defense against O.P.A.

The farmer who found an envelope in his mailbox containing money for a calf a meat-hungry city dweller was stealing, who promptly went out to the pasture and shot the "thief."

Scarcity of lumber in the middle west because of a shortage of cars to bring it from the western mills where it was piling up, and a scarcity of lumber in the west because it was needed in the middle west and the mills were on strike. Favoritism in selling, so that a home owner had to pay a carpenter fifty dollars to put in a two dollar plank because the lumber yard would only sell to the carpenter; so that the personal friend of the grocer could buy shortening, while the average customer was told there was none.

Selling a thing for ten times its value because someone is in dire need of it. Forcing a man to buy something he has no use for to get something he needs. Stupid little things.

But little things like atoms make an atom bomb, when there are enough of them. They must be separated, and the evils allowed to dissipate, to prevent the explosion. When they are brought together...

THE man who shot the President was never found. The papers insisted that it must be a communist who acted on orders from Moscow. That seemed hardly probable, and certainly Russia took no advantage of the situation, so if the deed was directed from Moscow it was a meaningless, senseless act.

There was no way it could have been prevented. He insisted on taking his walks each day. To have adequately protected him would have meant evacuating a fair section of the Capitol city each day, while he took his exercise.

It was February twentieth, a cold, bleak morning. At eight A.M., almost to the second, as the President was walking along a sidewalk, his shoes making crunchy sounds in the hard packed snow, he suddenly stiffened, then toppled slowly forward.

The bullet was a high-powered, steel-jacketed one that entered just above the heart, breaking a rib as it plowed inward to the heart. Death was instantaneous.

Up until that instant no one had realized what a governor he had been on the flywheel of the growing juggernaut of unrest in the country.

From that instant on the wheel ran swifter and swifter. Two days later a judge who had been strict in black market cases in a Midwestern city was shot, and the next day retail dealers all over that city sold to the highest bidder.

The death of the President seemed to give a certain class of society the idea. The death of the judge seemed to crystallize the idea. In the two weeks following the President's death twenty-six judges and federal men were slain.

The squatters league formed in Chicago and immediately spread to other large cities. Organized bands moved into vacant houses and apartments and defied the authorities to oust them.

Unions defied authority completely, without a President in the White House.

Thousands of sex maniacs and petty criminals ran amok. Police forces were inadequate.

A temporary President was appointed from the Cabinet to serve until one could be elected.

On May first the unions began to enforce the use of fight cards. Thousands went into unions to keep from starving, but other thousands took to organized robbery, religiously leaving money to pay for what they took.

The temporary President was helpless and finally was forced to put several of the larger cities under martial law, and operate almost two thirds of the nation's factories under military control.

Finally, on July twenty-fifth, he resigned his office. The next day the army declared martial law. July 26, 1948! This story has been told before—of how the army arrested union leaders and took over their bank accounts and books. Of how the army, with its thousands of disgusted G.I.s shot over three hundred men in three weeks before resistance to martial law ended. And of how the national economy slowly but surely was restored under the sane decisions of men with the strength to enforce their will on the renegades in black markets and small monopolies all over the country.

But the story has not been told of the silent drama going on underneath the people's feet, as the atom-powered mammoths of sub America moved irresistibly here and there, carving out passages ever deeper.

The cubic miles of crushed rock taken out were being dropped into the many chasms discovered along the way, and hoards of geologists and mineralogists and engineers were studying the structure of the rock through which the machines bored their shafts.

PLANS for the new Capitol southwest of Chicago to house the surface and the sub-surface governments had been laid before the President's death. It was planned eventually to cut off the sub-surface group entirely from all contact with the surface as soon as it became self-supporting, but until that time it would be wise to have both sections of humanity controlled from a central point, Washington, D. C., was too far to the east for practical purposes.

The army welcomed the excuse for dictatorship, as it ensured greater safety through partial censorship of the press, and made it possible to eliminate individuals who threatened the secrecy of the project.

The President had objected to dictatorship as being fraught with too many potential evils. Yet he had dreaded the possibility of his defeat in the next elections and the possibility of a man coming into office who would reverse his decisions and possibly decide to reveal the whole thing to the public. Stalin had urged a military coup directed by the President. The British had urged sterner government to end the unrest and inflationary tendencies in the United States.

In the end things had worked out this way anyway, because they had to. There was no other way. Stories of races facing impending doom, and voluntarily ending their existence by the humane method of not having children are all very well—in fiction. Or if the entire race is doomed. But when a part of the race can be saved, too small a percentage would voluntarily choose extinction of their line in favor of others, and it would be those who chose extinction who should be saved, because they would have the highest qualifications that should be preserved in the surviving remnant in order to give the future generations a heritage of true civilization.

True civilization is not made of machines and technologies, although it may be dependent on them for its very existence. True civilization is made of ideologies and philosophies and senses of values. It is based on respect for the dignity and rights of the individual, coupled with a mass responsibility for his welfare. It is based also, and equally, on the respect of the individual for the rights and dignity of the masses, the community and the government, coupled with individual responsibility for its welfare.

A country in which a senile, selfish house owner can demand the four years savings of a man who fought to preserve his safety as his rightful profit is not civilized.

CHAPTER EIGHT

JERRY climbed into the waiting taxi and sat back in the comfortable upholstering with a sigh of satisfaction. It had been many months since he had left Seattle.

First he had gone to Hanford to help with the designs of the atom motor for the borer. When the first one had been completed he had gone with it to Chicago and supervised its installation in the test model. From then on he had been in the field, watching the performance of the atom motors and suggesting improvements and refinements in design.

This had been most important, for the motor had to be so designed that no neutrons or radioactives could filter past the shields and contaminate the bores.

The work of improvement had gone on at Hanford, the main research being concentrated on more efficient shields and better neutron barriers. Such progress had been made that the atom motor had been reduced in weight from several tons to the weight of a diesel with the same horsepower.

Alloying of the radioactives had resulted in almost perfect consumption of neutrons, and the escaping alpha particles in the motor were stored in a pressure tank as helium.

But extreme care had to be taken at all times, for the escape of large amounts of neutrons would begin the fatal, endless, reversible reaction of neutrons and hydrogen, and neutrons and elements which resulted in more and more neutrons, until eventually the slowly growing reaction would become strong enough to destroy life, as it was doing on the surface.

The events of the winter on the surface, the death of the President, and the change in government, had had only a mild effect on him, as he carried on his absorbing task "down under" and gazed with wonder at the sights uncovered by the machines.

Now Jerry was taking a well-earned vacation. He opened the paper he had bought just before entering the cab. The date on it was September 7, 1948.

The front page was much different than it had been a year before. Then it had been full of strikes, war scare, meat shortage, and hysteria. Now it was what would have been called ultra-conservative then.

Crime news was banned, although news of divorces, lawsuits, fires, accidents, and almost every other thing except crime was just as freely discussed as ever.

Crime statistics had proven that publication of crime news and the importance it had held in the newspapers had been a major factor in encouragement of crime.

Strangely enough most of the news concerned the doings of various religious leaders.

But Jerry was not interested in what was going on the surface. To him the surface was a foreign country, whose only interesting inhabitants were Catherine, Olly, and Alex.

He folded the paper and watched the passing scenery. Seattle had changed not at all during the past year. There were few old cars on the streets and lots of new ones. The taxi he was riding in was a '48 Dodge. And aside from the fact that all policemen were army men, the country looked and acted like the good old U.S.A. of the thirties and twenties.

The cab passed over the University Bridge and turned right toward University Way. There it turned left and went through the business district, and on to fifty-third, where Olly still kept the old apartment and his laboratory in the back of a street level store.

Jerry had not been permitted to wire ahead that he was coming, nor would he be allowed to say much of anything about his work. Correspondence with his brother and with Catherine had been difficult because he could not say anything about his surroundings or his work. The only things he could write about were comments on what was written him.

THE cab drew to a stop in front of the old, familiar door that opened onto the stairs to the upstairs apartment. Jerry got out and looked for change to pay his fare while the driver retrieved his bags from the trunk compartment and placed them on the sidewalk.

Then he unlocked the door and held it open with his foot while he picked up his bags.

Olly wasn't home, but the apartment looked the same as always. Olly's book lay on the desk in the living room. It looked nice with its dark green back and the embossed title in gold. NATURE AND ORIGIN OF LIFE. And under it in smaller letters, Oliver E. Chadwick.

Jerry recalled Olly's last letter in which he had hinted at something big. His words had been:

"When you get home I have something REALLY important to show you. A surprise that will thrill you as much as it did me."

Jerry looked around curiously, hoping he would see something different that might be this big surprise, but everything was the same as it had always been. Even the wastebasket seemed to be the same, and have the same papers in it as it had had in the Fall.

The sound of the street door opening came up the stairs. A rapid clatter of feet followed. Jerry listened for the sound of Olly's dragging footsteps to follow those of the first. Then Olly was standing in the doorway, a look of surprise and delight on his face, his figure upright and straight.

"Jerry!" Olly exclaimed. "When did you get here? Why didn't you let me know you were coming so I could meet you?"

"Olly, you old son of a gun," Jerry said. "So this is the surprise. You—you're all right now?"

"Yes," Olly answered. "That's the surprise I told you about. Nerve grafting made such advances since last year that it was possible to have an operation to correct my paralysis. It happened only two months ago."

"Darn it," Jerry exclaimed, tears in his eyes. "Gee I'm glad it was possible. Now you can play tennis again. How about a game this afternoon?"

"Well," Olly said with a sly grin. "If you can get Catherine to come along we might make it a foursome."

"Don't tell me!" Jerry laughed. "Olly, the old hermit finally has a girl. Or are you running around with one of your rabbits from the lab?"

"No, it's a mouse," Olly smiled. "And what a mouse!" He looked thoughtful, then added seriously, "You know, when I was all wrapped up in pity for myself I was blind to the fact that there might be someone who cared for me. And all the time that teacher who helped me so much in my notes, who I thought was the intellectual type, and only interested in my work, was really interested in me. It didn't dawn on me until after the operation."

"You mean Betty—" Jerry snapped his fingers in an effort to recall.

"Yes," Olly said. "Betty Tryon."

"Just a minute while I call Catherine," Jerry said. He rapidly dialed her number.

Her exclamations of delight at the sound of his voice could be heard across the room from the phone by Olly, who grinned appreciatively.

"She's coming over," Jerry said when he finally hung up.

It seemed only a moment later that her rapid footsteps came on the stairs and she ran into the room. In the doorway she paused, then walked forward casually, a twinkle in her eye.

Pretending to notice Jerry, she said in mock surprise.

"Oh, hello, Jerry. Have you been away? I've missed you lately."

"No," Jerry replied, looking thoughtful. "I guess I've just been out when you were over. I've been rather busy the past few months."

Then they were in each other's arms, and she was mussing his hair and kissing him alternately, and making up for all the lost months during which she had missed him.

"How's Alex?" Jerry finally asked.

"He hasn't been feeling too well," Catherine replied with a worried frown. "His heart is getting weaker, and he has to watch himself more and more or he gets too tired."

"I want to see him," Jerry said. "Suppose you drive me over to the campus and drop me off. By the way, will you help me beat Olly and Betty at tennis this afternoon, Cathy?"

"I shore will," she answered in a hillbilly voice.

"What time were you and Betty going to play?" Jerry asked Olly.

"At three o'clock. That okay with you two?"

"Okay by me," Catherine replied. Jerry nodded his acceptance, and the two went down the stairs, hand in hand.

SEVERAL new buildings that had been under construction on the campus in the Fall were now finished. Jerry looked at them approvingly.

School would open in another three weeks, and already there were many students on the campus, as Catherine drove the car along the drive that circled the library, parking it just behind in a space reserved for faculty members.

"I'll wait here," she said.

"Okay," Jerry replied. "But I don't know how long I'll be. Your father and I have a lot to talk about."

"That's all right," Catherine replied. "I've a book with me that I can read."

Jerry cut across the lawn to Physics Hall and took the steps two at a time to the second floor where Alex had his office.

When he opened the door Dr. Topanov was sitting at his desk poring over his ever-present scratch sheets covered with equations. He did not look up until Jerry spoke. Then he rose hastily, an expression of intense pleasure on his face.

"Jerry, my boy," he exclaimed. "When did you get back?"

"Just now," Jerry answered. "What's this I hear about your heart going bad on you?"

"Oh, it's nothing," Alex shrugged his shoulders as though brushing off a minor irritation. "Tell me, how has the work been going? They tell me you have done a wonderful job in suggesting improvements on the boring machine and the system of disposal of rock."

Jerry blushed self-consciously.

"I haven't done any more than anyone else in my place could have done," he replied. "But it's been interesting work. Under the surface is a whole new world. We've uncovered mysteries that probably never will be explained satisfactorily."

"What kind of mysteries could they be, to have no explanation?" Alex asked.

"Well," Jerry began. "In one place we've opened up a cavern with a level floor and high ceiling. The floor area is almost a sixteenth of a square mile. The walls and floor are solid granite, very hard and without a single crack big enough to slip a thin knife into. No openings except the one we made ourselves in the solid rock. And it's eight thousand feet under the surface.

"In that cavern are skeletons of men and animals. At least we assume they are men and animals. The peculiar thing is that when put together they are the bones of men from the waist up and of some extinct species of goat from the waist down! Improbable as that seems, the upper leg bones fit into the hip sockets as though they had been there originally.

"There are ten of these skeletons. The bones are all there, although they were scattered around and mixed up, somewhat like they would be if they had been collected indiscriminately and then strewn around.

"How did they get there? That's the biggest mystery. The only possible explanation is that somewhere in the walls of that cavern is a sealed entrance that is carefully hidden. If so, we haven't found it yet.

"And are these bones the skeletons of some half-human species of creatures, or really a collection of human torso skeletons and goat leg bones? What makes that part more interesting is that the skulls of the humans have a brain case larger than any other on record. Not only that, on two of them the bony structure above the temples indicates that they had horns of some kind, although there were no horns present."

"Hmm," Alex said thoughtfully. "At what age do the geologists place the formation where they were found?"

"No age can be placed on it," Jerry said. "By that I mean that the cavern is in the heart of a huge solid formation that has undoubtedly remained much as it is today since the earth first cooled. There aren't any signs of tools being used to cut into the walls and floor of the cavern, yet it could not possibly have formed in the shape it is naturally, with an almost polished floor, perfectly level right up to the walls. It looks like it might have been a huge, rough cavern that had been partly filled with water, and the water frozen and then turned into the same kind of rock as the walls."

"Very peculiar," Alex admitted. "I'd like to visit this place sometime. What are the other mysteries that have been uncovered?"

"THIS is the most unbelievable one of all," Jerry began. "In the same formation, but about fifty miles from the first, there was the same kind of a cavern, only smaller and with rooms. No openings from it of any kind. And in one of the rooms—there were six, in all—was found some kind of an electrical machine.

"At least we assume it's an electrical machine. It has coils of silver wire, but no signs of insulation on them. Any insulation of a resin or cloth variety would have vanished completely anyway after a few thousand years.

"Also there are things that must have been some kind of metal-cased vacuum tubes at one time. And here we had a chance to estimate the age of the thing."

"How's that?" asked Alex.

"Different metals were clamped together. In several thousand years the molecules of each would creep into the other. When they are of different metals this creep can be determined, and by comparing it with the creep in metals from the ancient tombs of the Pharaohs and other data we have, it is estimated that the machine is over three million years-old!"

"What is the machine supposed to do?" asked Alex. "Of course you and the other technicians didn't rest until you had examined it in detail and deduced its principle."

"As nearly as we have been able to make out so far," Jerry said, a note of exasperation in his voice, "the thing has no principle and can't do anything. We've even built a duplicate with insulation where it is supposed to be, and tubes specially built to duplicate the old ones, and nothing happens."

"Well, surely," Alex objected, "if it has coils and wires and vacuum tubes it has a circuit, and the elements of the circuit should give some hint of its purpose…"

"You would think so," Jerry said. "But the natural deductions from the circuit don't make sense. The motif seems to be opposing magnetic fields. There are dozens of small coils wired together and placed so that two electrically produced magnetic poles are together. These are in banks, so that they make plane disks of thin but intense magnetic opposition. The planes are about a thousandth of an inch thick and a foot in diameter."

"How are these magnetic planes placed relative to one another?" asked Alex.

"There doesn't seem to be any sensible relation among them," Jerry said. "That's the trouble. We have a machine that took at least intelligence to build, which has no discernible function except to make magnetic planes in circuits affected by vacuum tubes very much like our own radio tubes in construction, and the machine is found in a cavity in the heart of solid bed rock where anyone would have to pass through at least half a mile of solid, unbroken rock in any direction to get in or out. It would suggest fourth dimension travel if that weren't absurd."

"Perhaps so," Alex said thoughtfully. "Sometimes I wonder. There is a whole book of things that, on the face of it, are absurd and unexplainable. That's Fort's book, you know. And now it seems the unexplainable extends even into the Earth's crust. What else have you found?"

"Oh, lots of things. Too many to tell them all now, but I'll have a couple of weeks before I have to go back," Jerry said. "Tell me, Alex, how has your work gone?"

"It seems as hopeless as ever," Alex answered, his shoulders sagging at the return of the despair he always felt now at the realization of what was in store for the world.

"Tell me about it," Jerry suggested. "All I can say that you don't already know is that there is nothing new to tell," Alex replied.

"Tell me anyway," Jerry asked. "Just to refresh my mind."

"Well, all right," Alex gave in.

"AS YOU know, the concept of critical mass led to the atom bomb. In the materials of the atom bomb we have an atom disrupting due to a strike by a neutron releasing more than one neutron in the disruption. That makes additional neutrons which can disrupt other atoms in the lump. But if the lump is small most of these neutrons escape into the atmosphere, so that there is no rapid consumption of the atoms in the mass. That is where we overlooked things."

"I know," Jerry replied. "We just simply neglected to examine carefully ALL the things that happen to the neutrons that escape. The atmosphere is certainly a critical mass for anything. If any kind of chain reaction could be carried on in it by the simple turning loose of a critical amount of neutrons it would with certainty, and it IS. *We just assumed that the escape of a neutron put it beyond any need of attention.*"

"As you know," Alex went on, "The neutrons and radioactive atoms left over after the explosion of the atom bomb immediately began a secondary phase of activity like the first chain reaction of the bomb, only almost imperceptibly slow. Some of the chain reactions ended with the production of alpha particles, which ended the chain, for all practical purposes; but some of them ended with more neutrons than they started with, and some ended with the same number, but emission of hard radiation, such as is the case with the reversible chain reaction of hydrogen, which produces neutrons, deuterons, protons, and their corresponding atoms.

"In theory I could figure out the atmospheric composition that would end the process by cutting down the rate of production of neutrons in the various chains set up by the explosions of the bombs. There is no possible change in atmospheric content that could do this without the introduction of inconceivable amounts of finely divided solids, in almost atomic dusts, which would absorb the neutron production and convert it to alpha particle production.

"The most efficient system I have figured out yet would necessitate the spreading of fifteen million tons daily of atomic dusts in the stratosphere for over a century, of kinds that are either not available in sufficient quantities or are poisonous to vegetation in the amounts that would settle to the surface.

"It's simply beyond the ability of Man to stop the chain reaction in the atmosphere, and especially the stratosphere, that was started by the explosions of those five—no, six bombs, with the Russian one."

"And," Jerry completed the discourse, "in three centuries the atmospheric temperature induced by this radioactivity will reach a hundred and fifty-five degrees Fahrenheit, the hard radiation striking the surface will become lethal, and there will be a perpetual blanket of steam in the upper atmosphere that will completely hide the surface of our planet just as it does Venus."

"One thing I've re-examined very Carefully," Alex added. "There were always neutrons in the atmosphere. Why hasn't this reaction begun long ago? I have the data on that now. It's the critical density of neutrons. Below this critical density more alpha particles result. At this density exactly the same number of neutrons and alpha particles result, so that the reaction remains stationary. Above the critical density more neutrons result than alpha particles, so that the radioactivity of the atmosphere increases more and more rapidly until the substance of the atmosphere changes into alpha particle-producing atoms, when it dies down again.

"One atom bomb wouldn't do the damage. Two might. Four or five certainly would, so that my original work on the problem still stands. There is no loophole."

"Well," Jerry said with a sigh, "Catherine is waiting outside in the car. Are you ready to go to lunch, Alex?"

"I guess so," Alex replied, taking his hat off the old-fashioned hat tree by the door. He paused before opening the door and turned around to look at Jerry. Then he said, "If there were some way to increase the percentage of carbon dioxide in the atmosphere to better than sixty percent for a while we could end this menace. But burning all the estimated coal deposits and all the vegetation on earth wouldn't produce enough."

The two walked wordlessly down the hall and to the car. Alex's breathing was audible and slightly wheezing as he climbed wearily into the front seat beside Catherine.

THE housekeeper opened the front door as the three walked up the front steps of the Topanov house. She was smiling broadly, and her table, already set, expressed her glad welcome of Jerry with its assortments of steaming foods.

During the lunch she bustled around, worrying over Alex, insisting that Jerry eat more, and otherwise showing that her eternal threat to quit unless things were done to suit her schedule was just a bluff, and always had been.

In the middle of the meal, during a long silence, Jerry started to chuckle.

"I just remembered my general handy man," he said by way of explanation. "He's a big, husky moron. His name fits him, too. It's Orvis. Orvis Oshiboski. He's a typical Hollywood conception of the dumb gangster type. But he's certainly likeable. I have no end of fun with him, because he always takes everything so seriously.

"He's from Spokane, and he got his leave for the same time I did. He has one of those flat faces, with a broken nose bent over so that it accentuates the flatness of his face, making it look like it had been placed against a flat board arid kept there while it grew."

He chuckled again to himself. "I wonder what Orvis is doing now?" he went on. "Probably basking in the pride of his wife and kids. I'll bet he's sitting in an easy chair and his wife is bringing him his slippers and fluttering around, fetching newspapers, coffee, and smokes."

Jerry glanced slyly at Catherine who returned his glance with a look that told him she would like to be doing that, too.

CHAPTER NINE

ORVIS was not at home basking in the lap of luxury. He was closeted with Billy Nugent, his old high school chum and fellow spy.

Billy was at the typewriter, and Orvis was telling everything he could remember of what had happened for the past few months. The pile of typewritten sheets beside the typewriter was growing as Orvis talked.

From the railway depot he had gone straight to Billy. After a short talk Billy had told him to go home and get some sleep and meet him in the morning. So now, Orvis had been talking for six hours, while Billy typed it all down.

At last they finished.

"What good is all this going to do now?" Orvis asked. "The democracy is ended and the army runs everything. What can the big shot in Washington, D. C. do about it? Nothing."

"Just the same," Billy answered, "He's willing to pay for the information, and maybe he can do something. If he can expose this whole thing to the public the people might revolt and throw out the army."

"I'll bet he gets shot instead," Orvis said gloomily. "I wish I wasn't in on this."

"Even if he did," Billy answered, "you wouldn't get mixed up in it because he doesn't carry your name in his files."

JOHNNY DAVIS' face held an expression of bafflement as he turned the pages of the report Billy, in Spokane, had sent him. His keen brain was trying to coordinate what they contained with all the things he knew. More and more things weren't making sense.

And more and more he was learning things he didn't dare broadcast. Finally he laid the report down and picked up a scratch pad. He wrote some questions on it.

Why are they boring all over the country and not just under the cities?

Why don't they inform the public of the findings of strange relics under the surface?

Why are the bores down so deep, except under the cities where there are extensive bores that will serve adequately as bomb shelters, all completed with living quarters for millions of people?

Why are there carefully concealed passages from the upper to the lower levels of the bores—like the lower ones might eventually be sealed off permanently? He was thinking of Orvis' description of a heavy stone door that would drop in place in such a way that it would look like part of the wall.

Could it be...? No. He shook his head. The idea was too utterly fantastic. Or was it? He wrote the question at the bottom of the sheet:

Could there be some impending happening that would destroy life on the surface? If so, what could it be?

The question intrigued him. It would explain a lot of things. But there were also a lot of things it wouldn't explain. Why the secrecy? If the world were threatened by something that would make life impossible wouldn't it make life impossible in caves, too?

Maybe astronomers had sighted some comet headed toward the earth, whose tail contained poisonous gases that would kill off all life. Suppose it were predicted to strike in five or ten years. In that time caves to accommodate the whole population would be impossible to build, but enough to save part of the population could be hurried through in that time.

But if that were so, who would have the say as to who would be saved from destruction?

Johnny picked up the phone and dialed a number. After a short wait he spoke.

"Hello. Professor Harding? This is Johnny Davis. Could you tell me if any comet or other body is going to strike the earth sometime in the near future—say about two to ten years from now? Not that you know of? Well say, would it be possible for a comet to hit the earth and poison the atmosphere to such an extent that it would destroy life? It wouldn't? Oh, I see. Its tail is too tenuous. Thank you."

Johnny hung up. Now he was more puzzled than ever. The only threat that could come from the heavens was total destruction of the Earth, in which case caves wouldn't do much good.

The idea would be utterly screwy except for one thing. Why did the government ask the same question of all new recruits into the armed forces and into the labor battalions? Questions that dwelt on one theme—what you would do if you had to kill somebody in order to save someone else?

WHEN THE army had declared martial law for the nation it had put censorship on all newspapers and periodicals with the exception of properly incorporated clubs and their official bulletins, provided that their bulletins were not sold publicly.

Johnny had promptly formed the Scoop Reporters Guild, with at least three national scoops to your credit before you become eligible for membership. There were associate memberships to take care of the rest of his secret organization.

If he found some gigantic deception going on he could quite easily spread the news all over the nation by whispering campaigns. If there was catastrophe coming the people should know about it and have an equal chance to save themselves not just some chosen clique.

In case of a real emergency he would always send the news out over his regular newscast. Radio reporters were permitted to send without enforced censorship until they violated the long list of rules put out by the government, after which they were muzzled. Johnny had been very careful. Mainly because he preferred the army rule to the state of things it had supplanted.

A memory forced itself into Johnny's mind. He had been standing in the outer office. Doctor Topanov's voice had come through from the President's office, saying:

"What I have to say to you, Mr. President, should be said to you alone at this time."

"And Dr. Topanov is the world's top atom scientist," Johnny Davis said quietly to himself. "So that's it…" Rapidly he thought over in his mind the men he might pose this problem to, discarding them one after another. The government mustn't learn what he was thinking. If he were on the right track they would put an end not only to his investigation, but to his life—to preserve the secret.

If he could find the proof someplace himself and inform the public, they certainly couldn't kill everybody to keep the secret!

Half an hour later he was looking over the shelves of the physics section in the public library. He knew what he was looking for. It would be something about radioactives that could threaten the world. It must be connected with the explosion of atom bombs, the Russian bomb notwithstanding.

Finally he found what he was looking for in a book on atomic physics. He copied down what he thought essential.

"About 150 nuclear reactions have been studied and we shall now examine some general features of transmutation processes. In general the process is of the type:

NUCLEUS plus BOMBARDING PARTICLE yields NEW NUCLEUS plus ONE OR MORE—PARTICLES OF LOW ATOMIC WEIGHT plus KINETIC ENERGY.

"The phrase, 'particle of low atomic weight' implies a proton, a neutron, or an alpha particle. The disintegration may also be accompanied by emission of gamma rays."

Johnny whistled in amazement. A glimmering of the truth was seeping in. Disintegration might be like a slow, atomic fire. The production of more particles of low atomic weight than went into the process would imply that the process would increase—like a small flame in a pile of wood on a fire. All the elements of the atmosphere were subject to this radioactivity.

And the atmosphere was so great that the bombarding particles could not escape like they could in U-235 when it was smaller than the critical mass.

"So that's it," Johnny muttered to himself. "Undoubtedly Topanov figured out rates, based on the volume of atmosphere and found out how long it would be before this 'fire' reaches lethal proportions. Obviously that is what must be happening, or they wouldn't be building such elaborate underground caverns."

"Maybe there's something about critical volume of atmosphere," he went on with the thought. "Whatever the details, there must be a short period of safety left or they would be in more of a hurry."

Johnny left the library with the light of battle in his eyes. At last he had something to go on. In his mind thousands of facts were clicking into place. They added up to a picture that he felt sure was true, because no other common denominator could account for them.

He must handle it carefully, he was thinking to himself as he drove back to the office. A simple scoop over the radio might be ineffectual. The government would muzzle him—and issue a denial. People would do nothing. He must convince as many people—especially leaders in various organizations—as possible before the army discovered he knew their secret. Then even if they killed him the work he had started couldn't be undone. The public would know the scope of the coming apocalypse.

JOHNNY had not noticed the quiet, studious fellow that had been browsing among the books in the physics section while he was there. The fellow had been just part of the atmosphere of the library, to him, and so the secret service man had been able to see all the things Johnny looked up, and watch the expression on Johnny's face.

In his car as he followed Johnny later, he called his headquarters and reported that Johnny now knew the secret. They had known he would find out sooner or later. The secret service had traced the microphones in Chadwick's apartment and watched the men who had gathered the records. They had followed the records in the mails to Johnny's office in Washington.

Since then they had kept him under constant watch, and periodically gone through his files during the night, so that this moment would not arrive unnoticed.

Now it was time to act. What form the action would take would depend on Johnny Davis. For several months his broadcasts had been through delayed transcriptions, unknown to anyone except the operator of the radio station and the government man on duty while Johnny was on the air.

It went like this: Johnny would speak into the mike and his voice would go onto a recording tape. This tape would broadcast the voice ten seconds after it came from the mike. At the same time a loud speaker told what Johnny was saying, so that if he had managed to discover the secret and broadcast it without warning, his voice could be cut off the air while he was talking and before he could get any significant hints broadcast. That was the purpose of the ten second lag, which was short enough to go unnoticed, and long enough to take care of the first few words he might speak before the censor would realize what he was saying.

JOHNNY brought his car to a stop at a red light. The door of the sedan behind him opened and a man in a light gray suit stepped out. Just as the light changed to green the right hand door to Johnny's car opened and the man in the gray suit climbed in.

He was holding a badge in his hand where Johnny could see it plainly, so Johnny slipped the car into gear and said nothing to his visitor.

Through the rear view mirror Johnny could see the sedan still following, with three men in it. He took his eyes off the traffic long enough to size up the man beside him and ask:

"What's this all about?"

"Turn right at the next street," the man said by way of answer.

Johnny's mind thought over and discarded plans to escape. If he ran he might get away for a time, but without the organization that centered from his office he would be helpless to spread the news he had uncovered.

So he shrugged his shoulders in resignation and followed directions.

Fifteen minutes later he was seated before three men in uniform. They looked and acted like judges. One of them was talking.

"We brought you here," he was saying, "Because our field man saw that you had uncovered the big secret. It's useless for us to try to convince you your conclusions are wrong, so we'll start on the admission that they are right.

"But we want you to know the whole story," he continued slowly. "Then you may see why it IS a secret, and why you must keep it with us.

"In three hundred years the radioactivity in the atmosphere will increase to such proportions that no life on the surface will be possible. It will remain that way for two thousand years. After that time it will again be possible to return to the surface and go on where we left off.

"As you can see, this does not affect the present generation, or even the next couple, to any appreciable degree. And even with atom-powered earth borers we can't carve enough space under the earth to house the entire population of the world. So only part of the race can be saved.

"That's why we have to keep it secret. If it were made public the economic structure would collapse, and there would be struggles to see who would be the lucky ones who would be able to preserve their line. Fundamentally we are only concerned with saving the races of man, along with as many life forms upon which we are dependent as possible. It isn't quite the same as if our own lives were at stake. All of us will be dead long before disaster strikes."

"But naturally," Johnny said bitingly, "Your own children will be among the favored few who will find refuge while the people are left to face their fate unsuspectingly."

"Perhaps," the speaker replied. "What difference does it make whose it will be?"

"You have set yourselves up as gods to decide the destiny of the race!" Johnny said accusingly. "Why don't you put it up to the people?"

"You know what would happen," the spokesman answered patiently. "We would get misfits if it were left up to the public. We must select those who are civilized enough to live together in harmony, and educated enough to take their place in the work of survival. At first they will have the worst of it. They will have to remain underground permanently while the rest of mankind lives in freedom under the sun. They must be intelligent enough to realize they must stay there. In another fifty years a leave spent on the surface would contaminate their flesh too much to allow them to come back."

"Well, then," Johnny exclaimed, "Announce the thing to the world and let everyone take part in it. Then those who can't go below can exercise birth control to end the surface race."

"Which ones will volunteer to stay on top and exercise the birth control?" the spokesman said bitingly. "And how will you convince the millions who can't read, and the millions who would shove their mother aside to escape from a burning building, that they should have no children because in eight generations life will suffer agonies of radioactive burns?"

"I can see your point," Johnny conceded, "But I still say the public should have the say as to what will be done. They should be allowed to choose the method of selection and who is to enforce it, military dictatorship or not."

ONE of the other three army men spoke up.

"You could help us a lot, Mr. Davis.

Your program wields a lot of power over the public, and you have used that power carefully so that it has increased rather than waned during the changeover to army rule. Would you give us your word not to divulge what you know until you have had time to weigh the arguments pro and con?"

"And if I won't?" Johnny asked, his voice soft and dangerous.

"It would be too bad," the officer said slowly.

"I think I'll call that bluff," Johnny said. "I don't think you would dare lock me up. If you did it would advertise that freedom of the press is gone for good. Even if the people never found out why I was put out of the way they would imagine reasons just as bad, and act on them."

He glared at the three men for a moment, waiting for an answer. When none came he turned on his heel and walked out. With each step he expected to feel a hand on his shoulder, and the words telling him he was under arrest. But he reached the street door unmolested, crossed the sidewalk to his car, and climbed in.

Two blocks away a man stood on the street corner watching. His eyes followed every inch of the progress of Johnny's car. Finally, when Johnny was still half a block away he took off his hat and scratched his head.

Half a block down the side street a heavy sedan that was double-parked burst into life. Its motor roared, and it started up with a terrific burst of speed.

Johnny was over half way across the intersection when the sedan, going about fifty miles an hour, swerved and struck his car right at the driver's seat.

The man on the sidewalk stood still, looking at the scene of the crash with an expressionless face. The driver of the sedan climbed out and looked in at Johnny's crumpled form. Then he stepped back.

His eye caught that of the man on the sidewalk. He nodded once. Grimly. The man on the sidewalk turned and walked up the way Johnny had come. The "accident" routine had been used before. It would be used again. And again and again.

Was it right? The man shrugged his shoulders fatalistically. Perhaps there was some other way. But it was not for him to decide. His job was to follow orders. And logic says it is better to kill one innocent man to save many than to let him live so that later the many will die.

The fact is, such logic depends on a judgment that if the man lives the many will die, and if the premise is false the conclusion is criminal.

Only by actually letting the public know the truth could it be determined whether it would be wise to let the public know. And if it weren't wise there could be no recall of the error. It would be impossible to blot from the memory of the millions the knowledge of the doom coming to life on the surface. Perhaps it would prove impossible to keep it from them in the long run anyway.

CHAPTER TEN

JERRY stepped out of the "taxi" and through the doorway into the large lobby of the officers' "hotel." Its location was designated on the maps as "Hdqtrs. Sec. K; Level H; Zone G."

This meant that it was seven thousand feet below sea level and a mile and a half directly south of St. Louis.

His leave was over, and for the next four months he would be busy doing his job in this gigantic project of carving out living space for a nation under the surface.

Aside from the fact that there were no windows, the hotel was very little different from one on the surface. The lobby floor was of polished tile in various colors. There was an elevator bank along one wall that would take one to any of the seventy "floors." The hotel had ten thousand rooms and a bath for each room.

The plumbing was of copper tubing, and the sewage pipes led to a sewage disposal plant a mile or so away, where the solids were salvaged for use in the hydroponics gardens now under construction, and the water, after multiple distillation, was returned to the storage tanks.

Section K was the same as each of the other completed sections of the underground world; designed to be a self-supporting unit, housing a hundred thousand people and with enough vegetation to convert the carbon dioxide to oxygen, the vegetation providing food for the people and for the meat animals that would be needed."

Jerry had nothing to do with that phase of the work, however. His present job was to supervise the laying out of the subsection power plants. Their construction was a delicate, dangerous proposition. Boring machines carved huge tubes directly toward the center of the earth, going down until the temperature was high enough to produce high-temperature steam.

This could only be done where the rock formation remained solid clear to the core. Seismic probings didn't always show the true construction below, and several boring machines had been lost before they could complete their work, and the holes had had to be filled up.

But already three power plants were complete and in operation. After completion, the bores were plugged, with huge pipes leading from the plugs to the turboelectric power plants. Then water was admitted to the bore, to drop the thousands of feet to the level where steam would be generated.

Too much water would mean too much steam generated and then the plugs would blow, sending a gale of live steam throughout the underground world and burning all in its path.

The time lag from the admission of water to the buildup of steam pressure was very great, so that great care had to be exercised.

In the other direction, upward cooling pipes were imbedded in the rock, going up to just a few thousand feet below the surface. An interlocking valve system had been devised so that the water in the cooling system could go clear to the top without the tremendous pressure that would otherwise exist at the bottom of the pipes being produced. These were automatic, and worked themselves without power because of the difference in weight between hot and cold water.

The whole power system was automatic, requiring only supervising engineers to see that it stayed in operating order.

Each section would be built so that it would be much like a balanced aquarium, needing no replenishing in moisture, air, or vegetation.

As soon as one section was completed and manned by a skeleton personnel it was closed off from the construction areas around it.

Everything was systematized into unchangeable routine. There were now three thousand boring machines on the job, and several new ones being assembled each day.

Underneath Chicago had been built the gigantic factory section, where already most of the parts of the boring machines were being made independent of the surface factories.

The incredibly tough cutting tools that made up the forward jaws of the boring machines were the first part to be made in the new factory section. There were alloyed by an infiltration process after they were formed from a tough steel alloy. When completed they could chew out the hardest of rock for days with no sign of wear.

IN THE ten months since the first boring machine had poked its nose downward and started its slow, deliberate advance through solid rock, all this had been done. In ten years the job would be complete in its more essential outlines.

Then there would be room in the underground world for several million people.

A similar job was being done in Europe, Africa, Asia, South America, and Australia. In all, it was estimated that there would be living room for about two hundred million people where they could be safe for the two thousand years they would have to remain underground. Perhaps in that time they would not want to go back up.

There would be libraries, schools, gardens, and leisure to live a fruitful life of study and mental development in the caverns underneath the rough surface. Above there would be only hardship and work.

But that was a problem for the future, not the present. The present job was to make a place for as many people as the subsurface would permit, divorce them from surface life completely, and see that they were started in a peaceful, stable way of living that would ensure the preservation of the race indefinitely.

THERE were many problems involved in this work. Cavern cities could not be built where the earth would be constantly shifting for thousands of feet down, because there would be continual breaks in the tunnels.

Potential sections, under which the formation would not allow the construction of a powerhouse, could only be used for stockpiles, not people.

In some sections the temperature gradient was too steep for safe construction, and in others the nature of the rock was too fluid for safe structure.

In the sections where construction was safe the engineers had to exercise great care in judging how much space could be hollowed out without endangering the works. Stress patterns in the rock could be mapped with ever increasing accuracy, as experience with them grew.

When a new section was started by the borers, they made several test alleys—as they were called—clear through the section. From the walls of these test alleys the mapping of the stress patterns of the section could be made. Then the boring procedure could be mapped out and the boring done with relative security from mishap.

Much of the work had been shortened by the discovery of huge natural caverns in which living room could be built without the time killing work of carving.

Other caverns had come to light so that the cubic miles of material carved out did not have to be dumped at the surface.

The finest brains the country had were on the gigantic project, mapping each step of the way, foreseeing every possible contingency and allowing for it. The old industrial practice of the suggestion box for the workers also did much to increase the efficiency of things.

One laborer who had only a grade school education and no particular aptitude in any ordinary line proved to be a genius at figuring out synchronizing details. It was he who suggested the double barrier behind the borer, by means of which the boring machine with its atom motor would be always sealed off from the rest of the works, and yet allow the continual string of cars carrying the loose rock to travel uninterruptedly.

He had also designed the interlocking valve for the cooling system that permitted free circulation of water to any depth without buildup of pressure. With this second achievement to his credit he had emerged as an important person. The name of Steve Jensen went into the books as an outstanding figure in the building of the caverns.

Problem after problem in synchronization and coordination of all branches of effort was seen by him and solved, where it was not even seen by other men.

There were other men whose names became legendary in the history of the tunnel building. And among the most outstanding was Jerry's. Jerry had not been content with just his original assignment to supervise the operation of the atom motors.

He had redesigned the entire boring machine. The first ones had made a smooth bore, and moved along it with caterpillar treads pressed to the top, sides, and bottom of the shaft. Jerry had noticed a certain amount of slipping. He had incorporated a rifling action into the cutting and replaced the caterpillar treads with a worm that used the rifling, eliminating the slippage.

He had made the first bold plans to utilize the earth's heat to run the power plants, eliminating the danger of the original plan to use atom power.

He had studied the other branches of science brought into play in the construction of the bores. His omnivorous curiosity had made him part of every phase of activity.

AS JERRY stepped into the lobby of the hotel his mind was far away.

He was thinking of Catherine and Alex, and of Olly. The last thing he had done before leaving the surface had been to put in a request for them to be allowed to come down. If not to stay, then at least for a short visit.

Orvis rose from a chair, in which he had been half-asleep, and came forward to meet him.

"Gee, Jerry," he exclaimed, "Am I glad to see you!"

He took Jerry's bag and walked along beside him as Jerry made his way to the elevators. The elevator cage was circular in shape, being a new experiment. It rode on a cushion of compressed air, balanced by a counter piston of approximately equal weight in a counter shaft.

As the door closed the elevator shot upward at breath-taking speed. It braked to a smooth stop at Jerry's floor and the doors opened noiselessly.

The hallway was thickly carpeted, muffling the steps of the two men as they walked down it to the door to Jerry's apartment.

"Have a good time?" Jerry asked as he opened his door and stepped through.

"Yeah," Orvis said. "I bought that house on the south side that my wife had picked out. Boy, it's a honey. How'd things go, with you, Jerry?"

"Oh, fine," Jerry answered absent-mindedly.

In one corner of his room, wired together, stood the skeleton of one of the goat-man creatures Jerry had told Alex about. The others had been stored away to be placed later in the gigantic museum planned.

Jerry stood for a minute during his unpacking and gazed at it. To him it represented mystery. Mystery of an ancient race, and mystery of travel through solid rock. Mystery that exists beyond question, when there are such tangible proofs, but also mystery that may never be answered.

"Well, Orvis," he finally said, jerking his mind back to the present, "we're back in the harness again. When did you get back? Yesterday?"

"Yeah, yesterday," answered Orvis. "They want you down on section H. They said something about the gradient not being normal. They stopped work on the power bore two days ago, waiting till you got back to see about it."

"Did they say whether the gradient was too steep, or too flat?" asked Jerry.

"They didn't say," Orvis said slowly, "But I gathered they had stopped because they reached enough temperature before they went as deep as they should. I think they were afraid of starting volcanic action if they went deeper."

"Oh," Jerry said, relieved. "I was afraid for a minute they had a cold bore. Then there would be another section uninhabitable. We can't afford to have very many of them in the middle states, because lord knows there will be plenty of them on both the Atlantic and Pacific coasts."

"Well, you know what all the workmen from Pennsylvania said about section H," Orvis said gloomily. "They insisted there were people living in caverns there already, and we would have nothing but trouble."

"I know," Jerry said with a chuckle. "When we didn't find any they just said we hadn't gone deep enough. When we started the power bore they said it would be cold. Now it's too hot, so that proves there can't be caves farther down. The temperature at thirteen thousand feet or so is around three hundred, or they wouldn't have stopped the machine."

"Maybe," Orvis said darkly. "All I've got to say is: why, if it's so hot down there, do the rock chips come up cold? They come up hot from other bores much deeper."

"How do you know, Orvis? Did you see this for yourself?"

"Yeah. I was over there yesterday so that I could report to you when you came back."

"Well, suppose we go over and see now. I doubt if I could sleep with a puzzle like that in my mind." Jerry grinned in anticipation of returning to work. It was in his blood, as it always is with those who work in a continual atmosphere of danger and mystery.

THE elevator took Jerry and Orvis to the level where the trans-section railway station was located. Half an hour wait brought the Pennsylvania express, as it was called. They had no sooner been seated comfortably than the train began to move. A change of shift was going to work, so the cars were full.

Tunnels are peculiarly suited to high-speed travel. In this particular one, for example, the original twelve-foot diameter of the bore had been reduced to nine feet by an inner wall, behind which ran power lines, communication lines, water pipes, etc. This smaller cylinder broke off at the bottom of the bore to leave space for the tracks.

The trains were propelled by eight foot blades which not only bit into the air and pulled the train forward in the same manner as a plane, but they also piled up air pressure behind the train and reduced it in front so that the efficiency of the blades was much higher than they were for an airplane.

The train Jerry was on could go three hundred miles from a dead start to a dead stop in one hour without exerting its full driving power.

THE scene the two men stepped into at the Pennsylvania end was much different from that under St. Louis. There could be seen no trace of the naked rock. Plastered and painted walls, tile and rug-covered floors, and cool air conditioning made one forget that he was over a mile and a half under the surface.

Here the roughly hewn, circular tunnels with their rifling, the muted thunder of distant boring machines, the hot blasts of raw air, and the fever of activity made a different type of world.

Here was the frontier!

Jerry and Orvis climbed into an empty dump car and rode to the site of the power bore. It was at the lowest level, and could only be reached by dropping down the elevator shaft in a series of temporary lifts. The first dropped a hundred feet. Getting off that one, the two men used a ladder to climb down fifteen feet to the top level of the next lift, which took them another hundred feet lower.

Nearly an hour of this brought them to the bottom of the shaft, where another empty dump car took them to the top of the power bore.

Here the machinery was motionless. Its inactivity gave Jerry and Orvis a feeling of loss and insecurity that depressed them immeasurably.

The bore itself was four feet in diameter, with heavy spiral grooves that provided traction for the boring machine and the sections of bucket lifts. These bucket lift units were twenty feet in length, with an endless chain of buckets that picked up the loose rock and carried it to the top where it spilled into a trough. This trough in turn spilled the loose rock into the buckets of the next higher unit, and so on until the rock was carried to the top of the shaft. Here the trough spilled the rock into dump cars that carried it to the nearest dumping ground.

For this area the nearest dumping ground was fifty miles away, where a huge, slanting fault had opened some time in the remote past and left almost a cubic mile of unusable space open.

Jerry went over to the control panel for the bore machinery. The temperature meter connected to a thermostat near the nose of the borer showed that the temperature below was a trifle over three hundred.

"Where are the men that were on this job?" Jerry asked Orvis.

"They're over on the air conditioner section," Orvis replied.

Jerry went to a field phone on a portable board and gave the number.

The foreman on the job came over to the power bore in answer to Jerry's call.

After the first warm greetings and inquiries about news on the surface were over he explained what they had run into with the power bore.

"I don't know how to explain it," he said. "The temperature shoots up and drops with no rhyme or reason. On the last day we drilled, the temperature climbed to almost five hundred in the space of half an hour. Believe me we were afraid of an eruption. That heat at this depth could mean a rock flow. So we stopped drilling. When we stopped the temperature dropped back to the normal two hundred and ten at that depth.

When we started in again it began to rise again. You know the thermostat is so placed that no overheating of working parts of the machine can touch it."

"How far down is it now?" Jerry asked.

"It's eleven thousand."

"Orvis says that the chips coming up are cool in spite of the temperature registration," Jerry said.

"That's right," the foreman answered.

"Well," Jerry said, "put the crew back on and start in again. But move the control panel back and block the power bore off. Keep going until the temperature of the chips is that for the usual bore at the right depth, or until the machine melts. Frankly I think there's something rotten in Denmark about this."

"That's what I think," the foreman replied. "But I didn't dare go ahead on my own. I had to wait for you to come back."

"You did the right thing," Jerry agreed. "It's only two days lost, and they aren't really lost if you spend them on the air conditioned section."

CHAPTER ELEVEN

JERRY watched the temperature meter on the panel. Through the rock beneath his feet the muted rumble of the boring machine, far below, vibrated against the soles of his shoes.

For half an hour now the borer had been running. From the very first revolution of the cutters the temperature meter had begun to act up. Jerry watched the needle anxiously as it climbed toward the melting point of rock.

He frowned in perplexity when it dropped again for no reason. His perplexity grew when it again rose.

The foreman standing beside him said:

"See? That's just the way it was acting when I shut it off day before yesterday."

Jerry's only reply was a grunt. Suddenly, his face took on an expression of new interest. He saw something the foreman had missed.

There was a definite pattern to the rising and falling of the temperature! It was a pattern similar to a Morse code, and utterly unlike any sequence that might arise from the boring or the operation of the machine.

"Shut off the borer," he ordered. "I'm going down there and see what's going on."

Half an hour later the last bucket of chips reached the surface. Jerry began his descent, riding the buckets that now were empty, the brakes and motors cut out.

The journey into the bore was easy. Standing on one bucket and holding onto the fourth one up, his weight started the belt downward. Before it had gained much speed he was at the bottom and had hopped onto the platform, to repeat the process on the next belt.

Coming up he would merely signal for the buckets to be started, and he would ride them up the same way.

The miner's light on his hard hat cast sharp shadows of buckets and struts on the side of the vertical bore as he went downward.

Coast. Step off. Climb on. Coast. Step off. The repetition became monotonous as he went deeper and deeper.

He began to regret his haste in coming down unarmed. If he found what he expected to, he might better be armed. It wasn't too late to go back up and get some sort of weapon, but to do so would mean disclosure of his conclusions. The already active rumors about cave people in this vicinity would be given more fuel.

Somehow, Jerry thought, if there were men down below, they were probably intelligent. They wouldn't do such a senseless thing as hurt him.

The heat was growing terrific. Jerry's clothes were dripping wet. He knew that a thermometer would show close to one hundred forty.

At last, just sixty feet above the borer, Jerry saw what he had fully expected. The corrugated bore had cut through a tunnel in the rock. A tunnel that ran horizontally.

In this tunnel MUST be some creature that had a heat ray of some sort. A creature intelligent enough to figure out what part of the machine was the thermostat, and play the heat ray on it to signal to those above.

Why? If the creature were inimical he would melt the borer or jam the buckets. The buckets could be stopped by hand, without a heat ray.

Why the signaling—unless the creature wanted someone to come down and investigate?

Jerry stood on the bucket platform and looked half fearfully at the round opening a few feet below him. The light from his lamp drove the darkness away from the mouth of the mysterious tunnel. But no man, goat man, or any other living thing could be seen.

CAUTIOUSLY he lowered himself on the frame of the bucket section. The bucket line would have carried him past the opening too far from the lip of the side tunnel to hop off safely.

He dropped even with the ancient tunnel the power bore had intersected, then stepped into it. It was about four feet wide and seven feet high, with an arching ceiling and flat sides and floor.

The surfaces of the floor, walls, and ceiling were smooth, almost to the point of being polished. The tunnel ran in a gradual curve to the right, so that beyond a hundred feet it curved out of view.

The boring machine had gone through to one side so that one wall of the tunnel was intact. Yet nowhere could anything moving be seen. The floor for several feet from the breakthrough was strewn with broken rock from the boring operation, but other than that there was not a sign of anyone, or anything living, having ever been here.

Jerry kneeled and directed his light downward toward the boring machine. The light picked up a flutter of movement. An arm waved feebly, but no voice sounded. And the arm was bare.

Without hesitating, Jerry leaped the gap to the bucket belt and started down. As he went he shouted encouragement. Whoever was down here must probably be near death. The signals had been for help. NOT the calm signaling of an alien, underground creature.

Jerry hopped off the bottom of the bucket line onto the top of the borer. His light turned to the figure lying beside the thermostat box and a gasp of amazement mingled with horror escaped his lips.

The figure was that of a man of normal build, white skin glistening with moisture, and brown loincloth caked with rock dust from the borer.

The face, however, was startling in the extreme. Its expression was that of any man in great pain. The lips moved feebly in an agony of pain, caused obviously by the unnatural position of the right leg which was broken in several places.

But where the nose and eyes should be was nothing. That is, nothing but smooth skin. From the mouth the skin rose smoothly to cover a bald dome, interrupted only by a small, delicately formed ear on either side of the head.

The lips were normal in every respect, and had the capable fluidity of motion that comes only with speech.

"WHATEVER you are," Jerry exclaimed, "can you understand me?"

"Yes," the answer came in a low, resonant voice. "My leg is broken. I didn't see your bore and fell into it."

Jerry pulled off his trousers and started tearing them into strips.

"I'll make a rope of my trousers," he explained, "And strap you to my back. That way I can carry you up to where we can get this leg of yours fixed up."

The strange man said nothing. He had lain here for three days with a compound leg fracture, in a temperature of one hundred and forty degrees, or nearly that.

Jerry himself was growing weak from the heat. His head throbbed, and sweat blinded him continually.

And his eyes kept returning to that unreal nightmarish expanse of smooth skin where there should be a nose and eyes, and to the bald head that had obviously never been adorned with hair.

This was a man who must have been born under the surface, and whose ancestors for countless generations had been here. The implications of this being were more startling than the man himself.

Jerry's fingers trembled with excitement. What strange race had bred down below the surface, unsuspected except in superstition and the mad dreams of a few writers?

A thought struck him.

"How can you speak English?" he asked. "I don't speak English," the stranger replied. "If you observe closely you will see that my lips do not move. I am conversing with you by telepathy."

Jerry watched the lips. They were tightly closed in pain. A thin stream of some sparkling fluid had dripped from the lips to the strong chin.

During this exchange Jerry's fingers were busy. Now he tied strips of cloth into a harness around the stranger's shoulders.

At last he sat down with his back to the man and secured the strips around his own shoulders. Now he could rise and carry the man, and have his hands free for climbing back to the top of the bore.

Rising slowly he lifted the stranger so that he hung free on his back. Then he climbed to the foot of the bucket belt.

Putting two fingers in his mouth he gave a piercing whistle. Almost at once the buckets started to move.

The figure on Jerry's back slumped suddenly. The man had fainted. But there was nothing to be done until they reached the top of the bore. Then doctors and stretchers could be obtained, the leg set, and anesthetics administered to relieve the pain.

As Jerry hopped from the buckets to the first landing and felt the limp figure on his back sway, he thought, "I'm glad the poor fellow fainted. These hops would be torture if he were conscious."

"I haven't fainted," came the reply to Jerry's unspoken thoughts. "I've merely cut off body feelings. Self-hypnosis, I believe you would call it. And I would suggest that before we reach the top you cover my head in some way. Otherwise too many people will learn of my existence."

"They'll learn anyway," Jerry protested. "They know nobody is missing. It doesn't make any difference whether you look like them or like a dodo bird. You're still a sensation. By the way, there must be more of you where you came from. Can you tell me about yourself?"

"That can come later," the man said.

"You may as well know my name, though. I'm Lowahthy."

"I'm Jerry," Jerry said.

THE spot of light that had been a mere pinpoint at the start of the upward journey grew until at last the faces of the curious workmen could be distinguished. Half an hour after the journey started Jerry stepped from the bucket line onto the floor of the man-made cavern and willing hands relieved him of his burden.

In all the boring operations complete hospital units followed the workmen wherever they worked. No man was ever more than ten minutes away from a capable doctor, nurse and surgical equipment at any time, if they were needed.

So by the time Lowahthy had been lowered to a stretcher a doctor was bending over him, his unbelieving eyes darting from the fractured leg to the featureless head.

"We'll have to give him ether before I can work on him," the doctor said. He took the ether mask the nurse handed him, then paused in perplexity. How could he give ether to a man who had no nose and kept his mouth closed?

For that matter, how could the man breathe?

The doctor noticed a small puncture on the man's lower lip. A sparkling liquid was seeping from it. He bent over and examined the fluid. It was slightly green, and obviously neither blood nor any other normal body fluid.

Jerry was amused at the doctor's perplexity as he stood there with the ether cone and stared at the blank face.

"You don't need to give him ether," Jerry explained. "He's put himself in a state of hypnosis so that he can't feel any pain."

"Oh," the doctor answered, giving Jerry a piercing look. "Well, perhaps I'd better give him a shot in the leg anyway, just to be sure."

"NO!" The word screamed in Jerry's mind, and the doctor jumped and looked around, suspecting someone behind him had shouted.

"I don't think you need to do that, either," Jerry said. "Just forget about his feelings and fix up his leg."

"We'll have to take him to the base hospital to do that," the doctor said. "His leg will have to be set under a fluoroscope. It's broken in too many places. Probably have to use metal pegs to hold the broken pieces in place."

Two men picked up the stretcher.

"Leave the power bore alone until further orders," Jerry told the crew foreman, then followed the doctor and the stretcher.

CHAPTER TWELVE

TWO days later Jerry sat at the edge of a hospital cot, upon which lay Lowahthy, whose face was now relaxed and smiling.

Amazed doctors had set the bones in his leg and tried to analyze the sparkling fluid that coursed through his veins. That they had been unsuccessful did not surprise them, because they knew that a fluid that could take the place of blood successfully, and also make lungs unnecessary, would be beyond the present ability of chemistry to analyze.

"Hello, Jerry," Lowahthy said, although his lips did not form the words. "I want to thank you for saving my life."

"That's nothing to thank me for," Jerry replied. "Anyone would have done it. But—would you like to tell me more about yourself now, Lowahthy?"

"I think that's in order," Lowahthy answered. "There isn't much to tell, but I suppose it will sound like a lot because it will all be new to you."

He lay silent for a moment, apparently collecting his thoughts in preparation for his story. Then he began, so slowly that Jerry could not at first be sure it was not his own thoughts.

"Years ago I was a man just as you," Lowahthy said. "I had a nose and eyes, and breathed. I was born on the surface. The town doesn't matter, nor does my name as it was then.

"I belonged to a secret order whose name I am not at liberty to divulge. This secret order has existed since prehistoric times. It has never advertised, nor has it sought to increase its membership indiscriminately. Yet it is continually studying people for the express purpose of increasing its membership.

"There are a few 'front' orders affiliated with this group secretly and unknowingly, through which the initiate must go to reach the inner group.

"What I am going to tell you now must remain secret for many reasons. I'm not asking for a promise of secrecy, because you will be unable to tell what you know. If the desire to tell ever comes to you, a peculiar complex in your brain will make you forget what you know temporarily so that you will be unable to tell.

"Far under the surface—farther than you would think it possible to go, is an inner world. There light is ever present, but not light as you know it. It's light that makes itself known to the mind or spirit of man, so that he has no need of eyes, but can see directly with his soul.

"Also heat grows less after it reaches its maximum a few miles down, so that the inner world is comfortable. And down there many changes are possible to the body that could not be effected on the surface, or even here in these new caverns.

"These changes are only possible near the neutral center of a great gravity field. You of the surface have always assumed that when a field is neutral it ceases to exist. Thus you have studied positive and negative electrical fields and derived their laws of behavior, and then assumed that when they neutralized one another they ceased to exist.

"Far from that being the case, GRAVITY IS A NEUTRALIZED ELECTRICAL FIELD. And at the center of the earth, where the ATTRACTION due to gravity disappears completely, the gravity field has not disappeared. Far from it. There the behavior of matter as you know it is subtly altered, due to the slower and weaker motions that it experiences. Electrical fields are weaker. Repulsions and attractions are weaker, and molecules, once formed, are more stable. Also light travels much slower.

"THERE are natural caverns and tunnels leading downward to this center that were discovered unknown centuries ago by races that lived on Earth before Man was created. These races knew all the mysteries of science, and had vast laboratories in the core of the planet in which they probed into the mysteries of life and immortality. They are not there now because they have gone on to larger worlds where the gravity fields are greater, and consequently the effects at the neutral center of such a field more complete. But they left much of their knowledge and their huge laboratories with their human students, as a heritage from the ancient masters of the elder races.

"It is there, in those laboratories, that I gave up my nose and eyes, which I would no longer need, to preserve my sinus cavities permanently from dust and germs, and gave up my blood for the ichor of the gods, which would forever replenish the body tissue and preserve it from infection. It was there that the last atom of radioactive matter was drawn from my body tissue, and I was at last assured of flesh immortality! I still eat, although the amount of food I need would not keep your body alive. I still drink water, although I seldom need it, since I lose moisture only by perspiring.

"And in the years since this change was accomplished, my mentality has grown unhindered by bodily ills, until today I use my body only as a contact with materiality; able to roam the world and go from this planet to others in spirit, coming back to this body only as a bird returns to its roost."

Lowahthy became silent. In Jerry's mind pictures began to form.

He saw the goat men whose bones had been found in the cavern with no entrance. But now they were flesh and blood. They were members of the elder race. Not a mixture of goat and man, but a pure race developed on some far world in the dim past before the Earth had cooled and born life.

They were a strange race according to the standards of man. Growth to them was perpetual, as it is with the giant redwoods, or the ancient dinosaur. In mental power they were Man's equal, but surpassed him because of longer life. When Man is old and senile, losing his memory and mastery of things learned in his youth, a member of the elder race had just begun his mental growth and had centuries of development yet ahead of him.

Where Man is careless of the development of the average member of his race, permitting the less favored ones to remain in ignorance until they die, the elder race permitted fewer individuals to be born and took great care in their mental growth. To them a mind was the most important thing in existence, and they felt a tremendous responsibility toward it, to see that it reached its full power unwarped.

It WAS a grave responsibility, for the fully developed Elder had the secrets of powers that could create or destroy worlds and races. If any of them had grown warped in mental stature it might have meant terrible catastrophe. An Elder who imagined himself a god might attempt to assert his power over the others, and the struggle necessary to subdue him would inevitably bring about the destruction of many worlds and perhaps many innocent races of younger intelligences. So the responsibility toward the young was indeed a grave one.

BUT thousands of years ago that elder race had departed, leaving the Earth for the young race of Man they had created by an artificial mutation on a naturally evolved race that had the necessary structure to permit development of the latent mind; hands with adaptable fingers, and lips that could be used for speech.

They had not left, though, until they had formed an inner group of men who knew the ancient secrets and who would see that out of each generation there would be new recruits brought down to the inner world and taught its secrets.

Master surgeons there were the ones who replaced the heart with an imperishable pump, blood with ichor, lungs with storage sacs for perfect food and water; and otherwise remodeled the body so that it would be a perfect machine.

Jerry broke in on this telepathically induced vision to ask:

"Are there actually individuals who are thousands of years old down there? And what is the ultimate purpose of all this?"

The vision shattered and the "voice" of Lowahthy sounded.

"The oldest of us is only about five hundred years old. Even he will soon leave us, for after that length of time the spirit finds the body a hindrance rather than a place of refuge and security. When this stage is reached the body is left to die.

"Just as you—when you were young—played with toy construction sets, and later with small chemistry laboratories, and finally with huge cyclotrons and giant projects, so also a time will come when you no longer care to bother with these." Lowahthy's voice sounded far away and dreamy. "The time will come when your spirit will dwell on things you are not yet ready to learn. Things of the spirit and things of cosmic structure. Then you will be ready to desert this mortal body just as you at one time turned your back on the toys of childhood.

"The ultimate purpose?" Jerry asked.

Lowahthy seemed to ponder this question. For perhaps ten minutes he did not move.

"I know you don't fully realize the importance of your question," he said at length. "Perhaps you won't understand the answer I give. Let's just say I'm answering it to myself and you are merely overhearing. It's a question that I have studied long and never found the answer. Maybe even the elders don't know.

"It seems to our limited minds that there must have been a time in the universe when there was no single spark of life capable of thought as we conceive it. Surely, when a man is born there is one more spark of intelligence in the universe that wasn't there before. So perhaps there was a time when there were no intelligent entities, although it doesn't necessarily follow, since there are now infinities of hosts of beings, the least of whom are perfect beyond our understanding.

"The god, the philosopher, and the religious man have conceived as being the Creator is as nothing compared to these. The gods who have set themselves up to rule the hosts of the heavens, the gods who direct the courses of the stars in the firmament and guide the faltering spirits of man from his first fearful step into the Unknown until that far-off day when they, too, are as gods—are mere beginners compared to Those who have existed since before any Time man could describe. They were incredibly ancient eons before the Earth was born, and to Them the Time of the Earth is as a fleeting instant in their eternities of experience.

"What is the ultimate purpose? If anyone could know, it would be Them. And yet—there are those who claim to have asked Them, and They did not know.

"I think," and here Lowahthy's voice became reverent and hushed," that the ultimate End is a universe that is one vast Mind, devoid of senseless matter. An Intelligence made up of infinite hosts of individual minds completely in tune, one with another, so that they function as ONE while yet being many. And yet, even though that is my opinion, I know it is full of inconsistencies that refute its possibility. I know, too, that such an opinion has been entertained and discarded by Those beside whom I am but as a babe. And I know, too, that eventually I will discard that opinion and choose another. And that my understanding of the Ultimate Purpose will mark my grade of development forever. And that finally, when the Earth has become a dim memory in the Mind of the Universe, and you and I are far greater in wisdom and experience than either of us are now—perhaps I will conclude that there is no Ultimate Purpose. That if there were, there would eventually be a state of suspended development, forever in a state of stasis."

LOWAHTHY became silent again. Jerry's mind was whirling at the vastness of the thoughts he had been experiencing.

"Perhaps," Lowahthy went on quietly, "there is an inconsistency in the very idea of an Ultimate Purpose. Sometimes I can almost grasp the point in such a concept that defeats its own existence and makes it impossible of being. And then it eludes me and I feel a frustration and impotence. Then a Voice whispers from the depths of my mind that when I DO grasp that elusive understanding of the Whole, I will be ready to take wing and assume my place at the side of the Elders and the friends who have gone before me into the vastness of space."

He jerked his shoulders as if, by an effort, bringing himself back to the present.

"Do you have things that would help us end the threat of radioactivity on the surface?" asked Jerry eagerly.

"No." The answer carried a note of finality. "There is nothing that can stop that. And there is no need of my interfering with the way things are going. We tried to prevent it." There was a note of sad regret in his voice. "We tried to create public opinion that would prevent the use of atom bombs, and failed. We tried to get the atom scientists to see what would happen, but failed in that, too, until after it was too late."

"Are there lower caverns where the entire human race could go and be safe?" Jerry persisted.

"There are," Lowahthy answered, "but it is forbidden. If we were to open the lower caverns and what they contain, there are too many who would misuse the powers they would have. There are instruments with which the mind can be molded at will, and through which a man can see with another's eyes, and hear with another's ears. There are machines that will transport the body through miles of rock and set it unharmed, even on a distant world. There are machines that can carve out vast chambers in the heart of a giant stone without any point of ingress or egress. But the uses to which they may be put are fixed by the Elders who made them. And we cannot violate their wishes, even though by doing so we might save humanity.

"Humanity," Lowahthy said, almost defiantly, "is just a small part of the universe. It will exist only for a brief moment. Then it will be gone. Please understand me. I would lay down my life for the least of you. You saved my life. I owe my present existence to you. Yet I COULD NOT VIOLATE THE TRUST OF THE ELDER RACE AND TURN MY BACK ON THE RESPONSIBILITY THEY HAVE GIVEN ME, TO SAVE THE HUMAN RACE. It IS being saved, in part. Or rather, the inevitable destruction of the human race is being postponed a few more thousands of years. But the death or suffering of any individual is not as important a thing as you think. In the eternity of growth of the individual a whole lifetime of painful suffering is but as a fleeting ache that is soon forgotten. An ache that as often is for the betterment of the person as for his hurt.

"But enough of this." Lowahthy's voice carried a note of finality." I see that you don't understand my position. You think I have the power to save humanity and don't care to. Let's leave it this way; the power is there to save all of humanity, but I am only one against many like me. If I wished to help I could still do nothing. I would be stopped before I could get started. And I don't wish to start because I can see the eventual outcome of such a course, and know it would be far worse for those saved than if they had perished, as they will."

"You're mistaken about my understanding," Jerry said slowly. "You forget that I am one of those who is letting a part of the race face its doom unwarned, so that the ones saved can be safe."

"Yes," Lowahthy said apologetically. "I had forgotten that for the moment. I'm sorry. I would like to talk with you further in a few days if you will permit me."

Jerry grinned. "You took the words right out of my mouth," he said. He stood up and went to the door. There he turned and looked back at the strange man from the center of the Earth. The vacuity of features that seemed accentuated by the smooth skin that replaced the eyes and nose no longer seemed nightmarish. In some strange alchemy of the mind they had changed so that now they seemed the norm, and Jerry's eyes and nose seemed the trappings of barbarism.

Of one thing Jerry was now sure. There were more things under the sun than even Shakespeare had suspected he suspected. He closed the door behind him with a feeling that he would be very humble from now on. His achievements were no longer worth mentioning.

FOR the next three days Jerry was busy. His increasing responsibilities carried him to all parts of the underground system of tunnels, caverns, and transportation lines.

Mining operations were being begun in the areas under the western states, where huge underground deposits of copper had been uncovered. The power plants already in operation were being turned into a vast network of power, which could be utilized by any section of the underground that needed it.

Each night, as Jerry returned to his apartment, he looked at the skeleton of the goat man and saw, in his mind's eye, the living creature, a member of the Elder Race that had created his own race.

The mystery of immortality still remained. Did man have a soul? Jerry didn't know. Death was an unknown gateway to this mystery. Lowahthy talked matter-of-factly of spirits, his own included, wandering the star ways, and finally deserting their bodies for good. If that were so, then death was not a horrible spectre, but a release. Certainty on that score would naturally change anyone's attitude toward dying. But without certainty there was always the possibility that death was the end, in spite of all the beliefs of humanity.

Jerry had to admit that Lowahthy's story of being an ordinary man whose body had been revamped to make it into a more perfect machine must be true. It was highly improbable that evolution had produced a creature that was human in every respect except that it didn't have eyes and breathing apparatus.

Moreover, x-ray had shown Lowahthy's heart to be a platinum machine with no moving parts, something like the Lindberg Heart but with a more subtle principle of operation which involved no moving valves of any kind.

X-ray had also shown the lungs replaced by a large storage space containing several separate sacs which contained different fluids.

During the three busy days Jerry thought over questions he intended to ask Lowahthy.

Then, on the fourth day he again stood beside the bed of the mysterious man from the center of the Earth. The doctors had told him another day would see the leg strong enough to bear weight. The problem of what was to be done about Lowahthy once he could be on his feet again, and what was to become of the power bore that infringed on the tunnel of the strange man, had been shifted fully onto Jerry's shoulders—to be settled at this meeting.

But as Jerry stood at the bedside of his new friend he didn't know just where to begin. He wanted to know so much that he knew there just wouldn't be time to cover everything in a few hours. So he hesitated.

CHAPTER THIRTEEN

LOWAHTHY watched his puzzlement, mentally, for a minute, then said:

"I appreciate your predicament, Jerry. So suppose you just relax and let me cover as much territory as I can."

"Okay," Jerry replied with relief.

"First," Lowahthy began, "about what I will do. Tomorrow I will go back down the power bore and get into my own world again. Then I will seal off the tunnel and bypass it so that you can complete the power bore. After that there will be no fuss about my existence. I see that you have kept quiet about our talk of a few days past. There are only rumors, and those are only half-believed."

Lowahthy chuckled. Perhaps the only physical sound he was to utter in Jerry's presence, and his real voice had exactly the same qualities to the ear as his telepathic voice had to the mind.

"Right now," he went on, "those of the workers who saw me are not sure they DID see me. Their minds, unable to rationalize what they saw, are in the process of denying it. The doctors will file away their x-rays and notes, and soon forget them. That will be seen to.

"As for you," Lowahthy hesitated a moment, "Jerry, you will soon be in complete charge of the underground. You are to be president of the underground federation and guide its destinies for many years to come. I would like to invite you to go with me back to my world, but I know your place is here, and here you must stay.

"I see you have many doubts. Some of them I can't resolve. Others I can. I can't prove to you that you have a soul that survives death, because whatever proof I presented could be explained away in many ways, such as hypnotism. The evidence of others will always have an element of doubt.

"I CAN prove to you that you can leave your body at will. If you wish I will take you in spirit down to the center of the planet and show you some of its wonders."

Jerry smiled. "Perhaps I wouldn't believe what I saw. Could you take me into the future so that I can see what is to happen to us, and to the people left on the surface?"

"No," Lowahthy said slowly. "I could take you into my thoughts about a possible future, but the future doesn't exist. Only the present. With the permission of the Elders and my fellows I could show you a future, and then maneuver things so that it would almost certainly come true. Without their permission I couldn't interfere with the course of events.

"But there are so many details involved in a picture of the future. For example, radioactivity has certain effects on heredity. Survival factors are so complex that it isn't possible to see all of them. And some unforeseen thing might upset a whole theoretical picture of what is to come.

"It might be that the artificial mutation performed on the sub-race from which mankind sprung might be undone in fifty years by radioactivity, so that the old animal race might return again. It might be that some other race of animals or insects might attain dominancy in the world. Mankind might die out or take a minor role. To tell the future I would have to know exactly what effects radioactivity will have on every gene pattern of every animal and insect alive today. I would have to know every detail of the present and trace out every future relationship that will result from the present state. It may be that the surface world will find out what is going on under their feet and ruin all your plans, and the whole race go down into extinction. To know certainly whether or not that will happen I would have to know every detail of every mentality alive, be able to deduce every situation for the next couple of centuries, and, in short, have the development of an Elder God, which I haven't.

"So you see," Lowahthy said with a smile, "Prophecy is more than just casting a psychic eye on some All Knowing Source and reading it like a newspaper. I could prophesize that an accident will take place somewhere at a certain time, and then see that it does. I could prophesize that you will die on a certain date at a certain place, and then see that you do. Those are no more prophecies than for you to say you will do something, and then do it. Do you understand the impossibility of what you ask?"

"Yes," Jerry said. "I guess I have always looked at prophecy the way you say. I can see now how impossible it is."

"LIMITED prophecy is always possible," Lowahthy continued. "For example I could tell you the exact date and hour you will be married because I know, to an incredible degree—what's in your mind pertaining to Catherine. I could tell you almost the exact minute that your friend Alex will die, because I know every detail of his condition, and have much experience in the course of disease and organ failure in people. I won't, because it would affect your relationship with him.

"A future event is like the bottom of a funnel. If all the ingredients are already in the funnel it is possible to say a single event will take place at about a certain time—come out of the small end of the funnel. Otherwise anyone's guess may be more correct than my studied opinion."

"I can see that," Jerry agreed. "But could you show me what you think will be the future, knowing that I understand it is not infallible prophecy?"

"That would be a waste of time and *might possibly do harm*, Jerry. Suppose I told you everything would work out perfectly. You might relax and let what I say influence you detrimentally. Suppose I said there would be catastrophe. You might subconsciously feel it hopeless to fight against fate. Especially if several of my predictions came true.

"In answer to all the questions in your mind I will make several statements—and those will have to satisfy you. None of them will be concerning the future, except the one already made concerning the fact that you will eventually be in the highest position of service in the underground civilization you have helped carve out of living rock."

"Sometimes I wish I weren't able to see so well abstractly," Jerry said with a laugh. "You have convinced me of what I already knew, I guess. I can't know the future. I can't know if I have an immortal soul. Things will go on just the same as they would have if you had never been here. So I will accept your statements and make the best of them. Fire away."

"Very well," Lowahthy smiled. "First, man does have a soul. It comes into being almost exactly three months after the egg starts developing into the human baby. Once formed it can never be destroyed. If, for some reason, it is not formed, the body may develop completely but the child is born dead.

"Second, when you die your personality will remain intact, but the thing known as consciousness is altered. Rather, something is taken away from it that existed in the brain-functioning and not in the soul functioning. This alteration cannot be described so that any living person would understand it.

"Third, everyone eventually reaches the state of perfect development, although it takes longer with some, after death. The worst criminal eventually becomes a saint. The child born with a mind that is still blank when it dies will surely reach perfection of knowledge and development, too. So in the long run it doesn't matter that the children left to the mercies of the radioactive elements may die before they reach maturity.

"Fourth, the frame work of the individual's progress is his sense of values. As these change toward the time-proven ideal, the individual advances. Without a judgment as to relative value a decision cannot be made. Without a sense of values a judgment cannot be made. The sense of values of any individual is a tremendously complex thing. The play and interplay of this sense brings action, understanding, desire, ambition, and their opposites. The primary purpose of education should be to develop this sense toward the ideal. Moral law is a generalization of certain standard conclusions based on the experience of a race or of the hosts of the heavens.

"Thou shalt not lie. Thou shalt not steal. All the commandments are based on conclusion from what will surely happen. There is no such thing as sin or righteousness in fact. It would be better to call them by their right names: successful and unsuccessful ways of attempting something. It is as correct to say it is a sin to do some trivial task carelessly as it is to say that it is a sin to kill another man. Neither is a sin, and both are ways of avoiding trouble which *inevitably lead to more trouble than they eliminated.*

"THE vastness of the universe is beyond the ability of man to conceive. As far as the most powerful telescope can reach, that distance is as nothing to the distances through which the star clusters drift, and in which they exist. Light can travel forever without getting any nearer the edge of the universe than it was at the start, for there is no end to it.

"Age cannot be applied to the universe, because it had no beginning. As it is, so it always was and ever shall be. Billions upon billions of years from now you, Jerry, will still exist and be aware of your existence. The certainty of this fact should alter your sense of values so that no short-range expedient will seem desirable if its inevitable consequences are adverse. Just as you would build a house to last a lifetime, and not just a day, so also you should build your life to stand forever, and not just until death.

"Understand all these things and you will progress. Accept them as so, if you can't understand them to be correct, and in the end you will have progressed just as rapidly."

Lowahthy laughed suddenly. "I guess I've been preaching," he said. "But tomorrow I will leave you and perhaps never see you again in this life. You will know that far below, toward the center of the earth, I am still living, as are thousands like me. Our two ways are separate, yours and mine. Sometimes you may feel the probing of strange thoughts in your mind as I watch you through machines whose principles you should never try to fathom, lest in fathoming them you leave them for irresponsible children to misuse. The things you will do—the things you have already done—will ensure the perpetuation of the race during the reign of fire that is to cleanse the surface of all its past errors.

"In the end, when humanity once again makes its home on the surface, it will make the Earth a garden of Paradise, free of harmful germs and insects, free of weeds and filth, and rich in the things that are good for man. Keep that in mind as you make your decisions and plans."

THE next day Jerry accompanied Lowahthy back to the bore from which he had rescued him. Together they descended to the tunnel through which Lowahthy had stumbled.

There they solemnly shook hands. Each felt a great attachment for the other, and regretted the necessity for this parting.

Then Lowahthy turned his back and walked swiftly down the tunnel. He was soon lost to sight in the darkness.

Jerry looked after the departing figure long after it had disappeared. Then, feeling a great sense of loss, he slowly made his way back up the bore.

At the top he phoned the foreman to come and resume operations on the bore. Then he went on to his other duties. And his thoughts turned to Cathy. Lowahthy had said he knew when they would be married. Jerry chuckled.

His feeling of loneliness turned in Cathy's direction. He decided there was no reason to wait further. He would take a leave of absence from his work and ask Cathy to marry him at once. Then he would bring her back with him. And maybe Alex and Olly would come, too. Olly could find plenty of work that he would love in the hydroponics department.

CHAPTER FOURTEEN

IN THE beginnings of things time passes slowly. As they gather momentum time itself seems also to gather speed, so that at last the years brush by almost before they are noticed. It seemed that way often to Jerry.

The day he first read the Topanov-Chadwick Report, as it was destined to be named in history, took on the flavor of something in the dim remoteness of pre-history. The events leading up to the beginning of boring operations stretched out in memory so that they seemed to cover years of time.

The first year underground seemed an infinite period of attention to detail. Then, as things began to operate with less and less attention, and the hundreds of men under his orders became thousands, all capable and all knowing their job, the days took wings.

Marriage immediately took on the feeling of a dream of long ago. Two weeks after Cathy became his wife and was installed in his—their—suite in the underground, it seemed like something that had always been.

Almost before Jerry could take a breath they had been married a year. And, by a contradiction of the mind, almost before he could get used to the idea of being married he was a father of a strong-lunged boy.

Alex had lingered long enough to see his grandson, and then, one day, he was gone. A name in history. A memory to those who loved him.

Jerry loved to feel the pulse of the giant living thing that was the underground he had done so much to create. He knew personally more of the men who worked on the frontiers and stretched them farther and farther—north, south, east, and west—than any other single man.

Nineteen forty-eight became unexpectedly nineteen forty-nine...then fifty.

The radioactivity in the upper atmosphere was increasing measurably now. The time was drawing near when the inevitable would take place. Eventually the surface world and the underground would have to separate completely.

Meanwhile section after section of the underground was completing its quota and being declared a closed colony. One could travel hundreds of miles in any direction from Chicago and see nothing except completed works that would remain just as they were for the next two thousand years.

Jerry did not realize just when he became commander in chief of sub-surface operations. In June, nineteen fifty-one he became a five star general in the army. He regarded this rating as honorary, because he had never considered himself a soldier. There were other five star generals. These departed, one by one, for duty on the surface. Jerry was assigned their duties in addition to his own and thought nothing of it.

Then one day he suddenly realized that for several months he had been the only five star general in the underground. It came as a shock to him at first. Then he told himself it was only temporary. He paid a visit to the surface and found that officially he was in sole command underground. He went back dazed.

One of his secretaries brought him the official order with its "Whereas" followed by a long list of his achievements which he had hastily skipped over months before without realizing their significance, and saw that he actually was commander in chief of the underground United States.

He read it quite slowly. And as he read his amazement grew.

"Have I done all these things?" he asked himself as he read the list of his achievements.

THERE was his plan to split sections, so that when a new group of people came below they did not become segregated into a colony by themselves, but were spread out through the established sections, while old residents were chosen to fill the newly completed section. He had thought (out of a clear sky) one morning that it would be a good idea so that the newcomers could learn the ways of the underground from more experienced old-timers. He had jotted the ideas down hastily on a scrap of paper and handed it to one of the immigration chiefs later the same day.

What was so wonderful about that? Jerry shook his head in bewilderment.

There was a long list of changes he had suggested in every phase of construction and in every type of machine. The list was staggering. He realized for the first time how much he had done.

Much of it he hadn't realized at the time. Men had quietly asked him things while he was intent on something else. He had answered absent-mindedly and they had gone away. Then, days later he would be pleased to note that his suggestions had been adopted.

He had never become aware of the fact that his suggestions were orders, or that officially he was giving orders. He had never stopped to think that invariably the things he suggested turned out to be the best possible way of doing them. It had been like—well, like working a problem on paper that had no special significance. He just figured out the answers.

Now, suddenly, in the quiet of his office, he was realizing that more often than not the answers he figured out had been made into reality by the concerted efforts of hundreds of men working for days and months. And that just as often the results had become patterns that were repeated over and over again in each new section built.

And as the realization of how big a part he had played in the great undertaking struck him for the first time he grew afraid.

He was like a man who has shoved in his chips recklessly, thinking the game was for fun, and after winning is told he is rich. The thought of what might have happened if he had lost makes him tremble.

He was like a child learning to ride a bicycle, who goes merrily along, thinking his friend is holding him up, and then discovers that for some time he has been alone.

The realization of the future importance of his every command, the realization of the responsibility he had held for months without knowing it, and which he would hold in the coming months and maybe years, and KNOW it, caused him to tremble and be afraid.

"How can I do it?" he exclaimed aloud. "How can I make a decision when I know that my decision will involve the lives and the work of thousands and perhaps millions of people?"

"You have done all right so far, haven't you?" The voice sounded with startling abruptness. Familiar, yet strange.

Jerry glanced up, alarmed. No one had entered the room. They couldn't enter without his noticing it!

Lowahthy stood near the door, his lips spread into a smile, the blankness of his face seeming as always a blind spot in the vision rather than an actual expanse of skin.

"I'VE been waiting for this moment," Lowahthy went on hastily before Jerry could have time to get over his surprise. "And now I must tell you something you already know, deep down in your heart, just as you knew there could be no such thing as prophecy, and no conclusive proof that you, personally, are immortal, until you die."

"Whatever you tell me I will believe," Jerry said simply. "I know you can't be here. Yet you ARE here. I've often thought of you, and even at times imagined I could hear your voice."

"What I have to tell you is quite simple," Lowahthy said. "You have just become aware of your importance and it makes you afraid. So listen, and then you will be no longer afraid. How many of those achievements on that list are YOURS? Actually only one. The suggestion to put rifling in the bores so that the machine wouldn't slip as it cut. That was strictly your own idea, and a good one."

Lowahthy walked slowly forward and rested the palms of his hands on the desk before continuing.

"Some of the things on the list are my own ideas. Some are ideas of my companions far below, where we watched you from the very start. Some of the ideas on that list were first thought of by being out in space, for the welfare of Man is the concern of us all.

"Do you remember my saying that I could prophesy correctly only if I could get permission to see that my prophecy came true?"

Jerry nodded.

"We found in you, Jerry, a man completely sincere and devoid of self. At all times we have been with you and been an advisory council to you. You are not alone in your responsibility! You will NEVER be, so long as you remain as you are. Is it so surprising that the list of your achievements is imposing when you consider that it is the list properly belonging to minds far more experienced than yours, or mine? Some of them older in actual years than the human race itself?

"Do you remember that skeleton of a 'goat man' you used to have in your apartment before you were married? The bones in that once belonged to one of your advisory council! He is one of those who stayed behind to watch over the human race after the Elder Race departed. He is still here. And there are others—"

Lowahthy turned and pointed. Behind him, slowly emerging from a whirling mist that seemed to dissolve the walls and extend for hundreds of yards, was a host of creatures of incredible beauty and intelligence.

"Here is Sethantes," Lowahthy said, pointing to a Godlike figure whose high forehead carried a pair of horns that curved upward and held back a heavy thatch of black hair. "He it was who performed the experiment that resulted in the human race. Because he did that he must be forever responsible for Man until that day when Man is no more."

"And here is Apollo," Lowahthy said, pointing to a figure of perfection. "He it was who patiently inspired Man to stand erect and admire, beauty of form and strive for it. If it were not for him the human race would be much like the apes in shape. And because he is responsible for the present stature of Man he must concern himself with Man's welfare now."

"And see the others! Cpenta, Thor, Brahma, Po, Joshu, Moses, Capilya, Jesus and more than your eyes can encompass! You are not alone, Jerry! Look at them and never forget them, because when some problem comes up a small voice will whisper the answer. That voice will be from one of us. Remember that!"

AS A scene on a screen vanishes when the light is turned off, the scene vanished. Had it been real? Jerry didn't know. He smiled wryly as the thought of what Lowahthy had once said. It could be hypnotism, assuming Lowahthy had actually been present, or had been using one of his machines. Then, again, it could be just the product of his own mind, just as he had begun to think Lowahthy himself was.

What if it *had* seemed very real? Doesn't a dream seem real? That was it! He had dozed in his chair and his troubled mind, disturbed at the knowledge of his responsibility, had conjured up a dream that would provide something to lean on.

The more Jerry thought about it the more certain he was that it had all been a dream. The dissolving of the office wall to make room for the vastness of the gathering of images was definitely a property of a dream. That man with horns and legs like a goat was distinctly created by his own memory of what he imagined the hypothetical creature that had once owned those bones to be.

Yet—it was a comfortable dream. Already Jerry felt more at ease, and more confident of himself. After all, the hard work and the important decisions were all made. The underground was working perfectly, and without any more changes at all it could keep on going smoothly indefinitely.

Jerry chuckled to himself. His office boy could run things now, so what could he have to worry about?

Nothing.

He dismissed the whole thing from his mind. Now that he knew what even the stenographers had known for months, he would carry on the same as always.

"Guess I'll go see how Olly is doing," Jerry said to himself.

OLLY was bent over a microscope when Jerry entered the huge laboratory. His left hand was manipulating the vernier screws that moved the glass slide about under the eyepiece, and his right hand, as if belonging to a different body, was rapidly sketching lines on a piece of white paper.

Jerry had never grown used to Olly's ability to focus his eyes independently, one glued to the microscope and the other watching a piece of paper on the table. He knew that all good microscopists had this ability, and that anyone could get it with practice, but it always made his eyes ache just to think of it.

He glanced over the large room while waiting for Olly to finish what he was on. It was a room about fifty by a hundred-fifty-feet in floor area, and ten-feet from floor to ceiling.

Along the walls were shelves, incubators, and other equipment. The central area of the floor contained two rows of benches and vats, and among these laboratory assistants were moving or engaged in some work.

This was completely Olly's baby from start to finish. In its way it was as important as Jerry's work, because here all the forms of plant life on the surface were being studied with the end in view of preserving them so that they could once again be planted on the surface when the two thousand years passed.

"Hello, Jerry."

Jerry's eyes jerked back to Olly as Olly greeted him.

"Hi, Olly," Jerry answered. "How's the work coming?"

"Fine. Right now we're working on the pine tree. We have the gene pattern solved, and are experimenting with the cell types. We may be able to preserve the conifers on paper without keeping specimens."

"How can you do that?" asked Jerry.

"Well," Olly explained, "Already we have determined that three of the cell types in the pine are identical with three in the vegetable types that will be grown in hydroponics. The only differences are due to environment. By that I mean the type of sap the roots send up.

"Cell classification," Olly went on, "is like chemistry, only more complicated. In chemistry we have the molecule. One type of molecule will act different in different environments. For example, crystalline salt behaves differently than dissolved salt. Yet they are the same.

"In organisms we have cells. They react to their environments, and if the living cell is isolated from its normal environment in the organism and immersed in different baths, it behaves differently. We've found that cells that seem utterly different are often the same type. There are actually fewer cell types than there are different types of organisms, just as there are fewer elements than there are compounds. In the whole vegetable family there are less than five thousand different types of cells.

"The reactions of these cells to environment are incredibly varied. In the common geranium, for example, a cell that would ordinarily develop into a branch with leaves and flowers, when placed below the surface in water or moist dirt develops into a root. In the cockroach a cell that ordinarily serves as a muscle cell, when bathed in nerve fluid develops into a leg."

Olly pointed to a glassed-in room at the far corner of the laboratory.

"Come with me and I'll show you something I made."

JERRY followed him. Inside the chamber the air was stifling. A half-dozen strange plants were growing in a bed of black muck.

"Watch this," Olly said, touching a leaf of one of the plants.

The leaf recoiled and the whole plant stirred as if alarmed.

"This," Olly said, "is a strictly artificial organism. It has both plant and animal cells in it. It has a nervous system, a heart, and blood cells. Its skeleton is strictly vegetable. The result is something that looks like a plant, gets its nourishment from the soil and the light globe in the ceiling, and reacts like an animal."

"You aren't planning on revamping the human race to look like this, are you?" Jerry asked in mock alarm.

"Well—" Olly said slowly. "I was thinking of asking you if you would loan me your son for an experiment like this. I thought I might remake him into an intelligent potato or something."

"I have a better idea," Jerry said. "Why don't you get a son of your own and try the experiment on him?"

"That reminds me," Olly beamed, "The doc says I am going to be a father pretty soon now."

"No! Well, congratulations, Olly," Jerry exclaimed.

The three plants nearest to Jerry quivered in alarm at the loudness of his voice.

The two men left the hot room and returned to the bench where Olly had been working.

"What I'm trying to do," Olly said, his mind returning to his work, "is map a technique so that for the next two thousand years my successors can continue along the same lines. The development of artificial organisms can be made into a fine art. The science of mutation can be mastered so that new species can be created at will. It's not too far-fetched to envision a race of dogs, for example, that are as intelligent as men. Or a variety of plant with an intelligent brain. I've already made a plant with a nervous system. It can't reproduce, but it lives, and it's made of cells that reproduce themselves and adjust themselves into an ordered system that looks like a plant.

"You know, Jerry," he said slowly, "We are living in a very special period. The things we do now are like seeds. During the next two thousand years, while Man has nothing better to do and can't go anyplace, these seeds will develop. I sometimes wish I could come back in a thousand years and see what my work leads into. I really do. *The materials of life are being put into the same class as the raw materials of other departments. The art of making organisms will produce wonders we can't even imagine now."*

"Do you think it could be used to remake the individual man into a more perfect machine?" Jerry asked softly.

"How do you mean?" asked Olly.

"Well," Jerry hesitated. "Do you think, for example, that blood could be replaced by something better, if it's found? The ancient gods had elixir in their veins, you know. And do you think the heart could be replaced by something that would last longer? Something like the Lindberg Heart?"

"It might be possible," Olly said, startled at the thought. "I had never thought of all this in relation to improving the human organism. Such a thing would take time, of course. More time than I will live. The initial work would have to be done on different animals and perfected to the point where application to humans would merely be a routine application before it was even done the first time."

The two stood in silence for a moment, each deep in his own thoughts. Jerry was thinking of Lowahthy. Perhaps some day everyone would look like him, or at least have elixir in his veins.

Olly was thinking of the whole new vista for the future that his talk with Jerry had opened up.

"Well, I'd better get back to this specimen before it dies," Olly finally said.

"And I'd better get back to work myself," Jerry added.

CHAPTER FIFTEEN

THE break with surface America came in nineteen fifty-three. It was done by two simple directives. The first simply ordered the flow of people from the surface to the underground cancelled permanently. The second merely cancelled all leaves to the surface from the underground.

In the United States alone ten million people had gone underground. Eventually, if there had been time, ten times that number could have been accommodated, but the danger point in radioactive intensity was too close for comfort.

Probability is a wonderful study. For the single instance probability gives the chances of a thing happening a certain way. For the great number of instances it gives the rate at which things happen a certain way. With free neutrons in a given mass of matter of certain kinds, the probability of an increasing number of free neutrons being produced is less than one for a certain mass or volume, and a certain number of free neutrons. *But the probability curve climbs so that with a predictable number of neutrons in a given mass of material such as air the density of neutrons begins to increase instead of decrease.* And nothing can stop it. Nothing except partitioning so that volumes of matter are less than critical.

Therein laid the real safety of the underground sections. Radioactivity breakthrough into one section could be stopped by quarantine of that section. Geiger alarm units were part of every section of the ventilation systems.

On the surface the atmosphere could not be partitioned. The cancer of neutrons set free in the atom bomb blasts of forty-five and six had pushed the critical density above the stability level. In the beginning of this, the increase in neutrons took place at the rate of about a thousandth of a percent a month. By nineteen fifty-three this increase in neutrons took place at the rate of almost a tenth of a percent a month. By the end of the century it was predicted there would be mild, chance accumulations of radioactives in the atmosphere that would drift along and finally disperse again. At first these would only produce mild burns on those exposed to the rays. But as the years wore on and the density of radioactive elements in the atmosphere increased, these radioactive gatherings, or Geig storms, as they were to be called later, would become lethal in intensity.

In about three hundred years the mean density of radioactives would become lethal, so that nowhere on the surface could life continue to exist. In the oceans life would carry on for another century. Then, as radioactive energy raised the atmospheric temperature to the boiling point, the oceans would slowly evaporate and form a white blanket in the stratosphere where the cold of outer space would condense the colorless vapor momentarily, and gravity would grip the droplets of water formed and hurl them surfaceward to once again become steam.

Then, even life in the ocean depths would die out.

Jerry and the other technicians who had carved out the underground refuge for life had overlooked nothing. They had even foreseen that a day would come when the cooling coils near the surface would no longer work. When the atmospheric temperature neared the two hundred mark, and the first few hundred feet of the surface grew too hot to cool the circulating water in these coils, there would be no one left on the surface to interfere with their activities in preparation for the coming centuries.

Then grotesque figures in bulging, ray-proof suits would emerge from the underground and build giant refrigerating units. They were already blueprinted and the approximate date when their construction was to begin had already been set.

AVIATION would not become a lost art. In giant museums and in the pages of books stored below ground, every detail of knowledge of aviation would be preserved. And brief excursions by scientists into the stratosphere during the long twenty-century blackout of the skies would enable the race to keep check on the movements of the planets and the stars.

But aviation and astronomy would not be pursued to any appreciable extent. Instead, there were the arts of electronics, organism, music, writing, painting and the abstract arts and sciences to be developed to perfection. Two thousand years should see the growth of science into super-science, so that when the race finally climbed back to a surface once more friendly to life, the world could be made into a veritable Garden of Eden.

What of life on the surface at present, cut off from safety, still organized into civilized nations, and still containing the bulk of humanity?

It would go on as it had. There would be wars; perhaps even atom wars. It was possible that those left to their fate might even bring everything to naught by destroying the world in a gigantic war.

But as the Geig storms began to take their tolls there would be a retreat from the open fields, where food was grown, to the cities and surface caverns where the huge shields of masonry and stone would protect the dwindling populations from the searing blasts of miles thick concentrations of radioactives.

During these first years the death toll would be very great. The population would dwindle to a point where the food supply, whatever it turned out to be, would determine the total of the living.

And then, even they would go. There would inevitably be a last man, turning his bewildered eyes to the cloud-filled skies.

He will try to pierce the swirling, impersonal mists that hide from him the blue of the heavens above, and the stars he has never seen.

He will turn his eyes dumbly on his fallen mate and look uncomprehendingly at the white blotches of burned, dead skin that rays he could feel but not see had burned into her. He will wonder why she does not smile at him as she did a few brief minutes before, not understanding death.

And then, perhaps, he will turn his back on her, and wander over the horizon in search of another mate, or even a scurrying newt or a small weed so that he will not be alone.

THE LAST MAN
His dragging footsteps scrape the ground
Where once the clarion calls did sound
Of birds who graced the springtime air
With fluttering wings, and songs so fair.

With weary stride he climbs a hill
Once dense with life, but now so still;
Where once the crow made raucous sound.
But now his feet touch lifeless ground.

His footsteps falter; then he stops.
His shoulders sag, his young head drops.
His eyes look sadly o'er the scene
Where once was life and grass was green.

His eyes search o'er the naked plane.
They search in hope—but all in vain.
For he's alone and e'er shall be.
The last of all mankind is he.

His feet move slowly, then he's gone.
He wanders on, and on, and on,
Until at last when Life sinks low,
His footsteps falter and grow slow.

His dragging feet step on the sod
Where once men walked and worshipped God;
Where children played, and puppies romped;
Where cattle grazed, and horses stomped.

He wanders on in hopeless quest,
Not knowing it is all a jest
Of Fate, whom Man did think so kind
That She would never cease to mind.

Wait! What is that atop yon hill?
He cries aloud with child voice shrill.
And staggers as he hastens on.
But lo, 'tis gone. 'Tis gone! 'Tis gone!

The leprous sky now sears the land
Which once was sod, but now is sand.
No river winds around the hill.
Now all is silent. All is still.

No more shall children sing and dance.
No more shall horses run and prance.
No more shall flowers scent the breeze.
Nor shall their honey lure the bees.

No more shall dewdrops nestle where
There once were plants, for now Earth's bare;
Her children gone beneath the sod
Where once men walked, and worshipped God.

TEN years after the underground world cut itself off from the surface all news from the surface was banned from general circulation.

The rising generation would be better off without the influence of such news. Jerry's son was now entering his early teens. So were thousands of other youngsters. They had been born underground and had never seen the sun.

In fact, they had no desire to see the sun, other than the curiosity that would prompt a surface youngster to go to the circus to see the elephants. To them the surface was a hostile place where people were wild and unable to live together in harmony. It was a place where radioactives would enter the body and cause tiny, scarring burns in the tissue that would prevent waste products from being eliminated, so that the body would grow old before its time.

Even to the oldsters, the people who had left the surface when they were already men and women, the surface seemed to be something they had read about, rather than lived in.

None of them felt the least desire to leave their well-ordered lives where lack of interest in something was considered an illness, and where you went to the doctor if you didn't feel perfect so that he could decide which vitamin you were short on, or in what way you should correct your diet.

Disease became a curiosity, and a disease germ always made the headlines of all the papers and brought an army of bacteriologists, doctors, and engineers to the section in which it was unfortunate enough to be discovered.

Olly had become the head of the biology department of Chicago University, under Lake Michigan. From his graduating classes the students went into all sections and taught the science of organism, or went into the huge biological laboratories where the study of synthetic organisms was a giant enterprise, and mutation was rapidly becoming an exact science.

His courses were required in the study of doctors and surgeons. Biochemists were finding his teachings an open sesame to the discovery and production of more and more new substances.

In nineteen fifty-nine the first bank of milk glands from cattle started their production of rich milk from a liquid that might some day be perfected so that it could become an ichor of the gods, and course through men's veins in the place of blood. This liquid circulated through delicately adjusted tanks where it picked up the substances which the milk glands could change into milk, and at the same time replenish their own tissue.

It was a crude beginning, but promised much. Newspapers painted glowing pictures of meat factories where the choicest steaks could be turned out without the less desirable cuts, egg factories where hens' eggs could be made without hens, and other not so fantastic pipe dreams.

It was even being debated whether it was worthwhile to keep the large zoos of surface animals, and the huge botanical gardens where trees and shrubs and grasses and grains were being perpetuated. Would the race need all these, when they once again could emerge from their low ceilinged home? There were even some who predicted that after twenty centuries in the perfection of the underground no one would care to return to the surface!

AS THE years went by, invention and improvement of existing products forged ahead in the caves and lagged on the surface. At first there was an attempt at mutual exchange of new inventions; but the ideologies of the two worlds became too divergent.

Above ground living became standardized and invention turned to implements of war. Attempts at space travel were made, but with little success. Surface travel declined and travel by air took its place almost completely.

Things like refrigerators and automobiles and radios were standardized by the military government and ceased to improve. Invention turned to spaceships, and few were the men lucky enough to get into a field of activity where originality was permitted.

Beneath ground aviation and space travel were of course left completely alone. Education, creative work, and invention were the main pursuits of the bulk of the population.

Every man had the entire resources of the nation at his disposal insofar as he was able to put them to sensible use. Every man could have the full benefit of the educational facilities, because money played no part in what a person could have.

By nineteen sixty even the literature of the sub and surface worlds were incompatible, so that exchange became undesirable to both worlds.

And when nineteen seventy came all contact with the surface was cut off entirely. During the following thirty years the surface world went on much as it always had. Occasional wars made wrecks of some parts of the globe overnight, and then peace would return.

But war as it had been known previous to the atom bomb was no longer existent. Large concentrations of land and sea power were vulnerable to bombing, and wars were started and ended before any considerable number of troops could be mobilized for battle. So war reached the ultimate in simplicity. Those who were in its path died, while those it missed went on as though nothing had happened.

The Jones' of Tulsa, Oklahoma, and the Smiths of Butte, Montana, and the Myers' of Squeedunk, Anystate, went their peacetime ways, taking meat out of nineteen fifty model refrigerators made in nineteen seventy in government factories, riding nineteen fifty-three model town sedans made in nineteen sixty-five, and the news of the destruction of San Diego, Detroit, and the crippling of Chicago and New Chicago by atom bombs in the undeclared Federation War left their daily routine unaffected.

It was only in little ways that their lives were touched. Mrs. Smith's next door neighbor would whisper that the Ripleys, down in the next block had been ordered not to have any more children because their gene pattern had gotten mixed up, whatever that was. Maybe it was some new kind of a disease.

Mrs. Brown would come home from the hospital with the vague story that she could not bring her new baby home with her because it "wasn't right." No, she didn't get to see it and she was heartbroken.

Then there was the new epidemic eczema that was breaking out all over the country. Whole communities would break out with the skin disease, and the government was issuing a special salve for it to everybody. It was caused by some virus that lived in the air, but that couldn't be isolated.

As late as nineteen ninety-nine there were sportsmen fishing in the streams and hunting in the north woods during their vacations from work.

And Christmas, nineteen ninety-nine was the biggest in history, the last Christmas of the greatest century of progress ever known!

January first, two thousand A. D., was just around the corner. During Christmas week there was a hushed expectancy in the air, as if the beginning of another century would bring a visible change—something dramatic. When New Year's Eve came, this feeling changed subtly.

AT THE stroke of midnight the parties of loud, celebrating people were strangely absent. In their place were small groups, huddling silently on street corners or standing on rooftops, waiting for something that they could not guess.

These subdued gatherings existed all over the world. In Russia, Spain, China, South America, North America, they were all the same.

Rumor was rampant. Some unnamed country was going to make a try for world dominion. Christ was coming again because two thousand years had passed. The end of the world was coming.

None of these happened. Nothing happened. Yet, as January passed and February drew to an agonizing end, the worldwide hysteria increased rather than lessened. It infected everyone from the dictators and rulers of the nations down to the humblest workers.

CHAPTER SIXTEEN

CROP failures were the rule rather than the exception in two thousand, A. D. These were due to two causes. One, hybrid seeds were growing into ancestral plants. This failure of strain had been going on mildly for several years, but in the summer of two thousand every strain of grain and vegetable grown seemed intent on reverting to the wild stock from which it had originally sprung.

Thirty-eight percent of the pigs born that year were scrawny razor-backs, regardless of their parentage. Wheat averaged five bushels to the acre. Corn was almost completely a failure due to disease. Oranges were tiny and sour, apples were small and tough.

Potatoes remained unchanged in form and produced a bumper crop. Carrots, by some unpredictable whim of fate were unbelievably large and tender. Five pound carrots that were sweet and tender crowded one another out of the ground.

But in every country the total of crops was not enough to feed the population during the winter.

Reversion of strain to ancestral stock was not the only reason for crop shortage, however. The second, and perhaps most disheartening cause was the high death rate among farm workers. For some reason they seemed peculiarly susceptible to the strange eczema that came and went mysteriously. Thirty thousand farmers died in the fields while at work during the year.

Fifty thousand more were incapacitated by it. And thousands of acres of crops went unharvested, while other thousands of acres were harvested by the government with drafted workers from the factories.

The winter of 2000-2001 saw the fall of organized government. Starving people raided warehouses filled with food and guarded it with guns they took from the armies sent to overcome their resistance.

Peoples all over the world broke up into small tribes, raiding one another for food supplies, and even killing off their own comrades to make the food stretch further.

Few fields were planted in the spring of 2001. Almost none of them were harvested.

The last newspaper known to be published was the Seattle Press for July 18, 2001. Its headlines were OLYMPIAN GOVERNMENT SEIZES KENT BEAN CROP.

A small item on an inside page read:

"Giant cockroaches chase chef out of Olympic Hotel. A horde of large cockroaches, some of them almost two inches long, overran the kitchen at the Olympic Hotel Restaurant this morning, carrying off three bushels of carrots, and driving chef Johnson out into the street when he tried to protect the only food left in the once famous eating place. He states that the roaches seemed to come from a drain in the basement floor, pushing out the screen that covered it."

Another item read:

"Stay indoors. People who spend most of their time indoors are least susceptible to the dread eczema that afflicts most of us. Its cause is still unknown. It has grown to such proportions that it now kills more people than all other diseases put together."

IT SEEMS incredible that no one discovered the cause of the widespread "eczema" and the universal reversion to ancestral form of both plants and animals. It seems that the densest of mortals should have looked into the sky and seen the cause of it all. But there seemed to be a mental reversion to ancestral denseness in the people that kept pace with the accumulating evidence of radioactivity as the cause of it all.

People ceased to think beyond their own immediate needs. The fall of government and the rise of local groups at war with one another perpetually seemed to be taken without thought. It seemed immediately logical, so there was nothing to get alarmed about. Perhaps the beclouded minds of occasional thinkers wondered how it had ever been possible for whole groups to live in harmony, but for the most part the thinkers lost out to the more active doers and lost what food they had, and starved to the point where they had no time or inclination to philosophize on existing conditions.

This mental denseness was due in part to the general decline in education after nineteen seventy, and to the fact that what education there was consisted mostly of practical trade and technical subjects. With the end of democracy, study of government and history was confined to the more advanced military colleges not open to the public. And with censorship of news the knowledge of what other peoples were doing and thinking was cut down to a bare minimum.

The transition from large nations with powerful well-knit governments to complete disorganization and the eventual family group in a state of hostile truce with its neighbors, as it took place between the year 2000 and the year 2005, went entirely unnoticed by the underground.

It was Jerry himself who discovered it. On his hundredth birthday, June 14, 2019, he expressed a desire to listen in on some surface radio, just to see how things were going "up there."

He had retired from active life twenty years before, but he was still revered as the father of his country.

The long unused radio tower on a desert in Arizona had been hooked in a radio that was hastily put together, and most of the day was spent in trying to discover why the set wouldn't work.

It wasn't until several days later, after a flight over part of the United States, and the building of a transmitter to prove the receiver would work, that it became certain that no broadcasting station on the surface was working, and that organized government was dead.

At once plans were made to help the surface people as much as possible. With education gone and people living like savages, their bodies too polluted with radioactives to bring down below without infecting the caves too, it was decided to make Geiger counters and teach as many people as possible how to use them to detect Geig storms and also teach them where to go to escape the full force of the rays from the atmosphere.

Laboratories were built into the bomb shelters near the surface, where individuals could be brought in and examined for the effects of living in radioactive surroundings. Here attempts were made from time to time to de-activate their bodies so that they could be adopted into the race. Those taken in were soon sent away as being too far-gone mentally to do much with.

The "specimens" returned to surface life with stories about giants living underfoot. These spread, and with the physical proof embodied in the Geigs, brought about a gradual respect for the "giants" whenever they appeared.

LIFE expectancy on the surface had been seventy years in 1950, according to the records. Other records discovered in New Chicago disclosed that life expectancy had dropped to fifty years by the year 1995.

Observation by cavern scientists from 2023 to 2030 showed that the life expectancy had dropped to twenty-five years, and that the oldest surface man was probably no more than thirty.

At the same time parenthood was coming at the age of ten or twelve, and sometimes even earlier.

Exploration of the surface filled the newspapers with interesting items for discussion.

"With old age creeping down and crowding the age of reproduction lower and lower," many people would say, "will the surface race end by its individuals dying of old age before they are old enough to reproduce? Or will the race adapt itself and reproduce earlier than our ancestors could possibly have done?"

"Will the race die out from starvation first? Or will it die out because it can't reproduce early enough?"

The news that cockroaches had become a major source of food for people on the surface created only mild interest. Only a few of those who had first come down were still living, and many of these had never seen a cockroach.

The roaches of 2019 were six inches long and very numerous. Able to run at prodigious speeds, they raided the countryside, leaping twenty feet to land on the unwary field mouse, or, when small animals were scarce, systematically cleaning whole fields of every shred of vegetation.

At night they swarmed back under the cities, making the dried-up network of sewers their home.

JERRY died in 2022 at the age of one hundred and three. Just as his life had symbolized the spirit of a free, adventurous America as it had existed prior to the atom bomb, blended with the cool, analytical courage of those who boldly carved out a whole new world from stone and made it work, his death symbolized the promise—for the future of mankind.

On the surface childbearing came earlier and earlier. Under the surface it came later and later. On the surface old age crept down the years until children were old in their teens. Under the surface old age was becoming an almost curable disease, and life expectancy based on death statistics had crept up to near the century mark with no ceiling in sight.

The two branches of the race had diverged to the point where they could hardly be said to be the same species. Indeed, the giants of the caves did not consider the surface dwellers as being brothers. They looked on them as nineteenth century man looked on the pygmies of Australia, and eighteenth century man looked on the Negro races of Africa that he raided for slaves for his plantations.

The last man in underground America who had been born on the surface died in 2041. The event did not create even a ripple in the course of history. Years flew by.

In 2100 A. D. the generation of man on the surface had dropped to nine years and the life expectancy to eighteen. In the caves the generation had increased to twenty-eight years and the life expectancy to one hundred and seventeen.

In organism laboratories there were dogs over twenty years old with platinum hearts, no lungs, and elixir coursing in their veins.

And musical composition, advanced mathematics, and four years of logic were required studies in all colleges.

PART THREE

CHAPTER ONE

RON looked thoughtfully at his latest figure, drawn on paper. It was hardly the equal of the doodling of a twentieth century man with his mind on a telephone conversation, yet to him, for a moment, it was a masterpiece in which his mind's eye could see an exact resemblance to a roach lying on the pavement ready to eat.

He beckoned his wives peremptorily to come and look at it. Amy, Betty, and Mary obediently dropped their own pencils and trooped over to view his masterpiece.

They looked at it doubtfully and Mary asked, half fearfully, what it was meant to be.

Ron's proud grin faded. His eyes, which had been looking for the instant appreciation he had expected, turned back to the drawing.

Gone was the resemblance to a roach. There was nothing but a senseless jumble of pencil scratchings. His eyes rose from the paper and looked around at the smooth walls and the clean floor on which he sat.

They turned questioningly to the transparent glass wall behind which several students sat watching him. Youthful giants with quiet, intelligent faces and friendly, curious eyes.

But now something was missing there, too. The smooth walls and clean floor seemed like the foolishness of children. The magic of the invisible wall seemed unimportant, and the students behind it were less than human.

Ron knew, as he had always known since he came here, that these friendly giants with their pleasant magic were weaklings. The most hardy of them would not have survived a day in the shadow of the el. It hadn't mattered before, but his eyes clouded with tears of pity for these soft, friendly giants and homesickness for the daily thrill of catching the beady-eyed roach.

Most of all he missed being king of all he surveyed. The magic of a paper and a pencil were as nothing to the feel of a hook sinking through the hard back of a roach.

The queer tasting foods and tasteless capsules he was given to eat could not compare with the white, juicy meat of a freshly killed roach with its warm smell.

Sure he liked not having to keep a weather eye on the Geig for storms. But the eight-foot ceiling of his new home pressed down on his spirit.

He longed for the Loop, where he could gaze up at the sky and see patches of cloud beyond the tops of the buildings, and where sometimes he could sit just inside the protection of his building and listen to the wind as it picked up the dirt in the street and played with it, forming it into swirling vortices that it pushed along.

He missed his occasional excursions down to the lake where he could squat on the shore and watch the waves break against the rocks.

All that had real meaning. It was a man's world. This—Ron looked around with wide eyes—there was nothing here for him. Of what use was it to make senseless scrawls on paper and learn how to tell what they mean? Of what use was it to ride in cars that went faster than a man could run?

Ron dropped his pencil slowly to the floor and stood up. Oliver had just entered the space where the students were. When he glanced at Ron he smiled and waved a cheery greeting.

Ron frowned and beckoned for him to come through the glass wall.

Oliver took a suit off a hook on the wall and did so.

"What is it, Ron?" he asked. "You look like something's upset you."

"Nothing has upset me," Ron replied." I want to leave now."

"Why?" asked Oliver in anxious alarm.

"I can't explain it," Ron answered slowly. "I don't think you would understand."

"Tell me anyway," Oliver said softly. "I can try to understand."

RON noticed the flashing expression on Oliver's face. It was the same expression he had felt on his own face the day before when his son had asked him a silly question and he had given a crazy answer that he knew his son would think over seriously, and not suspect he was being made sport of.

He glanced at the dark-colored mikes on the ceiling that were sending his voice through to the students. He caught their carefully hidden smiles of amusement. He suddenly realized that they were amused that he could have the "conceit" to think he might know something their giant minds couldn't understand.

Ron's eyes grew cold with a sudden contempt for these soft giants. They were patient, plodding-insects. They were slow and stupid, like a roach that has been feeding well for several days. He knew that if he suddenly bent over and picked up his sharp pencil laying on the floor and plunged it into Oliver's soft belly his eyes would blink stupidly for a moment before the realization would sink in that he had been attacked.

He knew there were lots of things these giants didn't understand. His vivid memory recalled their reactions to his questions about where he would go when he died. They didn't believe what they said! They considered him in the same light that he considered his infant son.

"Tell me," Ron asked sternly, "What is the use of all this playing with pencils and books? What will it do for me?"

"Why Ron," Oliver said gently. "It will make it possible for you to learn many things. Your understanding will increase."

"If that is so," Ron said triumphantly, "why is it that you and those (pointing to the students who were watching with intense interest now) can't understand that I am a man?"

"We know you're a man," Oliver remonstrated. "But you must understand that life is more than just being a man. You must learn the mysteries of nature. You must learn the history of the past, and how to live with your fellow man."

"Then why don't you go to the surface and learn the thrill of catching a roach?" Ron demanded.

"That isn't necessary for us," Oliver objected. "Nor is it any longer necessary for you," he added.

Ron parried this with a blink.

"Tell me, Oliver," he asked, "what is the most important thing about living?"

"Why," Oliver hesitated. "I think that learning is the most important. Mastery of nature and understanding of all things, or at least as much of an understanding of all things as it is possible to get."

"Do you have that understanding?" Ron fired.

"Perhaps more than you think," Oliver smiled.

"And perhaps not," Ron answered. "Tell me, is there anyone among you giants that you don't like very well?"

"I suppose so."

"Why?" Ron asked.

Oliver frowned. "Perhaps because he is selfish and inconsiderate of others."

"And he can read?" asked Ron.

"Of course," Oliver said in mild surprise.

"Then why is he selfish and inconsiderate of others?" Ron asked triumphantly.

"Reading has noth—" A light of dawning comprehension appeared in Oliver's eyes. He looked at Ron with a new respect and Ron's heart beat faster at that look. It was the first time it had been given him by the giants, and on the surface anyone who did not give it met violence.

"I think I see what you mean," Oliver said slowly. "Yes. I really think I do. You may be right. It's so long since such problems were really problems down here that we have forgotten about them."

RON looked at Oliver puzzled. Oliver didn't notice this. He was looking at the students behind the glass wall. And in his mind he was seeing the same things Ron had seen a few moments before.

His eyes turned back to the child-figure that was Ron. He took in the self-reliance and self-confidence that could and had faced almost certain death carelessly to satisfy his curiosity. He noticed, perhaps for the first time, the capable bearing of this orphan of the surface.

He turned back to his students. Those qualities lay dormant there. They MUST still be there, or the race would go down. Would they last through two thousand years of easy living with nothing to test them? That was really a question. *Can courage last for a hundred generations if there is not a single event to bring that courage to life?* Can a man without thinking risk his life or invite certain hurt to his body if all his life he has been taught to avoid risk and danger, and his father and father's father before him have been taught the same thing?

How long could the qualities *that made a man* lay dormant without dying out? Ron had recognized that they were not here. Oliver had noticed the contemptuous way Ron had looked at his abdomen and the sharp pencil lying on the floor, and guessed the thought that had passed through Ron's mind.

He wondered. What would it be like to face physical danger? To him it was an academic question, but someday it might become very real to the race of man.

"I'll have to write a thesis on that question and see that the possibility is taken into account in our education system," he mused silently to himself. In the back of his mind a question insinuated itself. "Would our ancestors consider us sissies?"

"Well?" Ron's voice interrupted Oliver's thoughts.

"When would you like to go back to the Loop?" Oliver asked.

"Now," Ron answered, the vision of a square meal beckoning him.

"All right," Oliver said sadly. "But, Ron, would you come back sometime and see me. We are friends now, and I'll miss you."

A look of pity appeared in Ron's eyes, but he veiled them hastily so that Oliver wouldn't guess.

"Yes, sir," he answered.

RON sat on the curb, his small bare feet in the gutter, eyes aglittered with intense excitement. Beady, faced eyes appeared in the gloom, several feet down the circular well that yawned at his feet.

He stopped breathing, hoping that he smelled enough to entice the insect out of its hole. Firmly grasped in his right hand was a shiny, untried metal hook with which he hoped once again to catch a wary cockroach and drag its squirming body out onto the pavement. Then—how many lifetimes it seemed since he had REALLY had a good meal!

In the gloom of the street opening to the building at his back three female figures crouched, breathless.

A playful breeze sent dancing, miniature whirlpools of dust along the street. And overhead through the gaps in the el structure and the tall buildings, white clouds drifted lazily across a blue sky.

The soft murmur of waves beating against the shore of Lake Michigan bounced in echoing cascade from wall to wall of the buildings.

A distant roar that rose and died out bespoke the falling of another building somewhere, blocks away.

The cockroach hooked its front legs over the edge of the hole and sniffed at Ron's feet.

THE END

If you've enjoyed this book, you will not want to miss these terrific titles...

ARMCHAIR SCI-FI, FANTASY, & HORROR DOUBLE NOVELS, $12.95 *each*

D-1 **THE GALAXY RAIDERS** by William P. McGivern
SPACE STATION #1 by Frank Belknap Long

D-2 **THE PROGRAMMED PEOPLE** by Jack Sharkey
SLAVES OF THE CRYSTAL BRAIN by William Carter Sawtelle

D-3 **YOU'RE ALL ALONE** by Fritz Leiber
THE LIQUID MAN by Bernard C. Gilford

D-4 **CITADEL OF THE STAR LORDS** by Edmund Hamilton
VOYAGE TO ETERNITY by Milton Lesser

D-5 **IRON MEN OF VENUS** by Don Wilcox
THE MAN WITH ABSOLUTE MOTION by Noel Loomis

D-6 **WHO SOWS THE WIND...** by Rog Phillips
THE PUZZLE PLANET by Robert A. W. Lowndes

D-7 **PLANET OF DREAD** by Murray Leinster
TWICE UPON A TIME by Charles L. Fontenay

D-8 **THE TERROR OUT OF SPACE** by Dwight V. Swain
QUEST OF THE GOLDEN APE by Ivar Jorgensen and Adam Chase

D-9 **SECRET OF MARRACOTT DEEP** by Henry Slesar
PAWN OF THE BLACK FLEET by Mark Clifton.

D-10 **BEYOND THE RINGS OF SATURN** by Robert Moore Williams
A MAN OBSESSED by Alan E. Nourse

ARMCHAIR SCIENCE FICTION CLASSICS, $12.95 each

C-1 **THE GREEN MAN**
by Harold M. Sherman

C-2 **A TRACE OF MEMORY**
By Keith Laumer

C-3 **INTO PLUTONIAN DEPTHS**
by Stanton A. Coblentz

ARMCHAIR MASTERS OF SCIENCE FICTION SERIES, $16.95 each

M-1 **MASTERS OF SCIENCE FICTION, Vol. One**
Bryce Walton—"Dark of the Moon" and other tales

M-2 **MASTERS OF SCIENCE FICTION, Vol. Two**
Jerome Bixby: "One Way Street" and other tales

If you've enjoyed this book, you will not want to miss these terrific titles...

ARMCHAIR SCI-FI & HORROR DOUBLE NOVELS, $12.95 each

D-11   **PERIL OF THE STARMEN** by Kris Neville
             THE STRANGE INVASION by Murray Leinster

D-12   **THE STAR LORD** by Boyd Ellanby
             CAPTIVES OF THE FLAME by Samuel R. Delaney

D-13   **MEN OF THE MORNING STAR** by Edmund Hamilton
             PLANET FOR PLUNDER by Hal Clement and Sam Merwin, Jr.

D-14   **ICE CITY OF THE GORGON** by Chester S. Geier and Richard Shaver
             WHEN THE WORLD TOTTERED by Lester Del Rey

D-15   **WORLDS WITHOUT END** by Clifford D. Simak
             THE LAVENDER VINE OF DEATH by Don Wilcox

D-16   **SHADOW ON THE MOON** by Joe Gibson
             ARMAGEDDON EARTH by Geoff St. Reynard

D-17   **THE GIRL WHO LOVED DEATH** by Paul W. Fairman
             SLAVE PLANET by Laurence M. Janifer

D-18   **SECOND CHANCE** by J. F. Bone
             MISSION TO A DISTANT STAR by Frank Belknap Long

D-19   **THE SYNDIC** by C. M. Kornbluth
             FLIGHT TO FOREVER by Poul Anderson

D-20   **SOMEWHERE I'LL FIND YOU** by Milton Lesser
             THE TIME ARMADA by Fox B. Holden

ARMCHAIR SCIENCE FICTION CLASSICS, $12.95 each

C-4   **CORPUS EARTHLING**
             by Louis Charbonneau

C-5   **THE TIME DISSOLVER**
             by Jerry Sohl

C-6   **WEST OF THE SUN**
             by Edgar Pangborn

ARMCHAIR SCIENCE FICTION & HORROR GEMS SERIES, $12.95 each

G-1   **SCIENCE FICTION GEMS, Vol. One**
             Isaac Asimov and others

G-2   **HORROR GEMS, Vol. One**
             Carl Jacobi and others

If you've enjoyed this book, you will not want to miss these terrific titles…

ARMCHAIR SCI-FI, FANTASY, & HORROR DOUBLE NOVELS, $12.95 each

D-21 **EMPIRE OF EVIL** by Robert Arnette
THE SIGN OF THE TIGER by Alan E. Nourse & J. A. Meyer

D-22 **OPERATION SQUARE PEG** by Frank Belknap Long
ENCHANTRESS OF VENUS by Leigh Brackett

D-23 **THE LIFE WATCH** by Lester Del Rey
CREATURES OF THE ABYSS by Murray Leinster

D-24 **LEGION OF LAZARUS** by Edmond Hamilton
STAR HUNTER by Andre Norton

D-25 **EMPIRE OF WOMEN** by John Fletcher
ONE OF OUR CITIES IS MISSING by Irving Cox

D-26 **THE WRONG SIDE OF PARADISE** by Raymond F. Jones
THE INVOLUNTARY IMMORTALS by Rog Phillips

D-27 **EARTH QUARTER** by Damon Knight
ENVOY TO NEW WORLDS by Keith Laumer

D-28 **SLAVES TO THE METAL HORDE** by Milton Lesser
HUNTERS OUT OF TIME by Joseph E. Kelleam

D-29 **RX JUPITER SAVE US** by Ward Moore
BEWARE THE USURPERS by Geoff St. Reynard

D-30 **SECRET OF THE SERPENT** by Don Wilcox
CRUSADE ACROSS THE VOID by Dwight V. Swain

ARMCHAIR SCIENCE FICTION CLASSICS, $12.95 each

C-7 **THE SHAVER MYSTERY, pt. 1**
by Richard S. Shaver

C-8 **THE SHAVER MYSTERY, pt. 2**
by Richard S. Shaver

C-9 **MURDER IN SPACE** by David V. Reed
by David V. Reed

ARMCHAIR MASTERS OF SCIENCE FICTION SERIES, $16.95 each

M-3 **MASTERS OF SCIENCE FICTION, Vol. Three**
Robert Sheckley, "The Perfect Woman" and other tales

M-4 **MASTERS OF SCIENCE FICTION, Vol. Four**
Mack Reynolds, "Stowaway" and other tales

If you've enjoyed this book, you will not want to miss these terrific titles…

ARMCHAIR SCI-FI & HORROR DOUBLE NOVELS, $12.95 each

D-31   **A HOAX IN TIME** by Keith Laumer
INSIDE EARTH by Poul Anderson

D-32   **TERROR STATION** by Dwight V. Swain
THE WEAPON FROM ETERNITY by Dwight V. Swain

D-33   **THE SHIP FROM INFINITY** by Edmond Hamilton
TAKEOFF by C. M. Kornbluth

D-34   **THE METAL DOOM** by David H. Keller
TWELVE TIMES ZERO by Howard Browne

D-35   **HUNTERS OUT OF SPACE** by Joseph Kelleam
INVASION FROM THE DEEP by Paul W. Fairman,

D-36   **THE BEES OF DEATH** by Robert Moore Williams
A PLAGUE OF PYTHONS by Frederick Pohl

D-37   **THE LORDS OF QUARMALL** by Fritz Leiber and Harry Fischer
BEACON TO ELSEWHERE by James H. Schmitz

D-38   **BEYOND PLUTO** by John S. Campbell
ARTERY OF FIRE by Thomas N. Scortia

D-39   **SPECIAL DELIVERY** by Kris Neville
NO TIME FOR TOFFEE by Charles F. Meyers

D-40   **JUNGLE IN THE SKY** by Milton Lesser
RECALLED TO LIFE by Robert Silverberg

ARMCHAIR SCIENCE FICTION CLASSICS, $12.95 each

C-10   **MARS IS MY DESTINATION**
by Frank Belknap Long

C-11   **SPACE PLAGUE**
by George O. Smith

C-12   **SO SHALL YE REAP**
by Rog Phillips

ARMCHAIR SCIENCE FICTION & HORROR GEMS SERIES, $12.95 each

G-3   **SCIENCE FICTION GEMS, Vol. Two**
James Blish and others

G-4   **HORROR GEMS, Vol. Two**
Joseph Payne Brennan and others